RON LOVELL

DANGER

 *by the*

SEA

A LORENZO MADRID MYSTERY

FIRST Edition
Penman Productions, Gleneden Beach, Oregon
Copyright © 2017 by Ronald P. Lovell

All rights reserved under International
and Pan-American Copyright Conventions.
No part of this publication may be reproduced, stored in a retrieval system,
or transmitted in any form by any means, electronic, mechanical,
photocopying, recording, or otherwise, except brief extracts for the purpose
of review, without written permission of the publisher.
Published in the United States
by Penman Productions, Gleneden Beach, Oregon.

The events, people, and incidents in this story are the sole product
of the author's imagination. The story is fictional and any resemblance
to individuals living or dead is purely coincidental.

Printed in the United States of America
Library of Congress Control Number: 2017938672
ISBN: 978-0-9988968-0-9

Cover and book designer: Liz Kingslien
Editor: Mardelle Kunz
Cover photo credits: iStock.com
Chapter opener/end art credits: iStock.com
Back cover photo of Ron Lovell: Andrew Randles

PENMAN
PRODUCTIONS

P.O. Box 400, Gleneden Beach, Oregon 97388
penmanproductions.com

DEDICATION

To my mother, Verna Lovell, and my grandmother, Lora Bickerton.
The two of you made me what I am today.

❧ ❧ ❧

THANK YOU

Although the idea for Lorenzo Madrid is my own, neither he nor I could exist without the help of close friends, all of whom I want to thank.

- *Linda Hosek, for the idea of Maxine March. I filled in the fictional details of her life, but Linda helped flesh her out as a character and also saved her from death—at my novelist's hand—many times.*
- *Nick Sharma, for suggesting the plot of "Innocent," out of which grew the character of Lorenzo Madrid, and for being a great business partner.*
- *Suzie Ross and Karina Ramirez, for sharing details of their work as nurses in mental institutions.*
- *Juan, Eulalia, Daniel, Raffa, and Madeline Perez, for help with Spanish words and phrases and helping me become an "honorary Mexican."*
- *Liz Kingslien, my designer, who turns my words on paper into books that look wonderful from cover to cover, and for long years of our working together on many projects.*
- *Mardelle Kunz, my editor, who makes sure these words make sense and are spelled and used correctly. I owe her a lot for rescuing me from many plot and grammatical miscues.*

--Ron Lovell

To Jim —
"Read or be hated!"
A valued friend.

Regards Ron

*"**The sea lies all around us.** The commerce of all lands must cross it…. In its mysterious past it encompasses all the dim origins of life and receives in the end, after, it may be, many transmutations, the dead husks of that same life. For all at last returns to the sea—the beginning and the end."*

— *Rachel Carson*

❦ ❦ ❦

CHAPTER

AFTER SEVERAL YEARS OF PROFESSIONAL UNCERTAINTY and personal danger, Lorenzo Madrid hoped to be entering a period of stability and happiness. The key to both lay in the office behind the door he was now unlocking. The sign on the door in old-fashioned lettering—**Lorenzo Madrid, Attorney at Law**—described both a wish and a promise. By setting up a general practice, he was looking for clients with many kinds of legal problems, not the thankless and largely unpaid work he had done for so long in immigration law. Although he might take a few pro bono cases in the future, he needed to make money now.

The location of the office also suited his current mind set and financial condition. A modest two rooms with bathroom and storage space in a historic building above a few trendy shops on Third Street in Corvallis, Oregon, would be perfect. Another plus: he liked being near the campus of Oregon State University.

As he checked out the desks and chairs in both offices, he heard a hiss and a curse behind him.

"Shee-it! The Ritz it ain't!"

Lorenzo's legal assistant, Samuel Lincoln, had arrived. He wheeled a cart stacked high with boxes through the door.

"You'll get used to it, Sam," said Lorenzo.

A LORENZO MADRID MYSTERY

"Didn't see many Black faces on the street," he said, shaking his head.

Lorenzo picked up a box marked BOOKS and carried it through the door to his office. Sam followed with another one.

"Relax, my friend," said Lorenzo, smiling. "It's a college town with people from everywhere. You'll find a niche. Besides, I'm going to keep you so busy that you'll be stuck in here day and night working for me."

"Sounds good," said Sam, nodding his head. "I want to learn."

Lorenzo had met Sam six months before, when he had been hired by a Hollywood producer to review the contracts for the actors in a film he was making in Oregon. Sam was part of the deal to be Lorenzo's driver, assistant, and all around fixer. When that job was over, Lorenzo hired him to come to Oregon and help him in his law practice. Since Sam intended to go to law school, the work for Lorenzo would be invaluable to him. After a course in how to be a paralegal, Sam was ready to go.

The two worked together for several hours unpacking and organizing the office. Lorenzo's files from his old practice in Salem were stashed in the storeroom. He wanted to start fresh with his new clients.

That process would be easy because of his many contacts in business, politics, and the legal profession. He had been out of the state for over a year, but he was not out of the loop and had already received several inquiries from people who wanted to retain him. He laid the folder containing details of their legal problems in the center of his desk. First thing tomorrow, he would see what he could do for them.

"We need to eat something and get you settled into a hotel for tonight," he said to Sam, who dropped a box and wiped his face.

"Sounds good to me, boss."

Lorenzo picked up a phone. "Is this thing working?"

Before he could confirm it, the phone buzzed loudly, startling them both.

"Scared the you-know-what outta me," said Sam.

"Lorenzo Madrid," he said, answering the phone.

"Lorenzo, you probably don't remember me," said a woman's voice,

2

"but I need your help."

Never a good sign, and Lorenzo didn't recognize the voice.

"I'm afraid I don't . . ."

"Of course I can't expect you to know who I am by the sound of my voice," she said. "How stupid of me!"

He waited for at least a minute, expecting her to go on. He looked at Sam and shrugged his shoulders.

"And so, you called me to ask . . ."

More silence. Lorenzo turned on the speaker so Sam could hear.

". . . for my legal help? For a referral to another lawyer? I hate to be rude, but I'm just setting up my practice here in Corvallis, and I don't have a lot of time right now. It's late and I need to get . . ."

Loud sobs were all he could hear.

She finally managed to talk. "It's about my son, Tito. He's not really my son. He's kind of adopted but not officially, and that's the problem. They want to take him away from me, and I can't let that happen. I'm the only mother he knows and if he is sent back, they'll kill him or put him to work in some awful mine or something. Or make him a child prostitute. Oh my God, I can't let that happen!"

Sam was pointing to his watch and rubbing his stomach. Lorenzo needed to end this conversation because it was going nowhere that made any sense.

"Okay, Ms. . . ."

"March. Maxine March."

A few pieces of this puzzle fell into place with the mention of her name.

"You're Tom Martindale's friend. I remember him talking about you. You were the one he was arrested for killing, but you weren't dead."

By this time, Sam was paying close attention. His impatience and hunger had vanished.

Maxine had stopped crying. She blew her nose loudly before answering. "Yeah, that was me. Tom and I were close at one time, but we had a major breakup. I haven't seen him in years. You and he were—are—friends. Right?"

"Yes, good friends. We help each other out from time to time. As a matter of fact, I'm the one who got him out of jail when he was arrested for killing you." He paused and looked at his watch.

Sam sat down. He was, as one of Lorenzo's law professors used to say, "all ears."

"This is all very interesting, but I've really got to go. I hate to be rude, but maybe you can make an appointment and come to my office. Are you in Corvallis?"

"Portland right now, but I might be moving."

"Okay, here's what we need to do," he said. "Let me put my assistant on the line, and he'll set you up to come in. Give us a day to get the office organized. As I said, we were just moving in, quite literally, when you called."

Maxine March answered in a steady voice. "Sounds good. I'll have pulled myself together when I see you, I promise."

"Here's Sam." Lorenzo handed the phone to the young man.

"Hello Ms. March," Sam said in his most professional-sounding voice. "How may Lorenzo Madrid, attorney at law, assist you with your problem?"

CHAPTER

LORENZO SPENT THE NEXT MORNING looking for an apartment for Sam. Luckily, because it was the middle of the academic year, there were a few desirable ones available. Off-campus housing is impossible to find in September, but more units open up after students get their first term grades and some decide to leave school. He found a place that they both liked in a new development west of the OSU campus.

Lorenzo loaned Sam furniture, towels and sheets, kitchen utensils, and dishes, and bought him a bed; then he gave his assistant the rest of the day off to get settled.

"The rest is up to you, my friend."

"You got it, boss!"

Lorenzo drove downtown to his office and tried to call Tom Martindale. His old friend was now a best-selling author of crime novels. His career at the university as a journalism professor had been dealt a blow by the very murder charge that Lorenzo had helped him get dismissed. Even though he spent only one night in jail and was later cleared of any wrongdoing, his academic career came to an abrupt halt. However, the book he wrote about the ordeal was a big hit, and he made a lot of money.

"You have reached the office of Thomas

Martindale, author and lecturer," said the recorded message. "I am currently on a book tour in Canada. Please call my publisher if you need to reach me." End of message.

Obviously, Tom didn't really want to talk to anyone about anything. So Lorenzo found an old email address he had saved and composed a brief message to his friend.

Hi Tom.

I need to talk to you about a person from your sordid past. Maxine March contacted me for help with something involving her son? Stepson? Not sure who this kid is. At any rate, she's coming to see me tomorrow, and I need to know what you know about this. Did you and she have a kid? His name is Tito. Hope you can help. Am setting up a law practice in Corvallis, of all places. I'll fill you in when we talk.

Thanks amigo. *Lorenzo*

Lorenzo spent the next few hours organizing backgrounds for the people on his list of prospective clients. There was a patent matter for a successful inventor who thought his idea for a wine dispenser had been copied by someone who had worked for him. There was a bitter fight between the sons of a wealthy manufacturer who had just died and the man's last girlfriend, who claimed to be entitled to half the man's considerable fortune. And, finally, there was a brief phone message from an old friend and former lover, Thaddeus Sampson. Thad was an attorney in the Oregon Department of Justice who had helped him several months before with a man Lorenzo was trying to get into the Witness Protection Program. He called Thad immediately.

"Thad Sampson."

"Is this the most handsome Black man in Oregon state government?" said Lorenzo, laughing.

"The very same, if you're the man who looks like Antonio Banderas used to look."

"Yeah, he's no longer the knockout he once was," said Lorenzo.

"All those years with Melanie Griffith have taken their toll. How are ya, kid?"

"Good, good. But dying to see you, pal. I heard you just opened a practice in Corvallis. What's up with that?"

"It's a long story. We need to get together and catch up."

"Yeah, man. Indeed we do."

"But I gather you called about a legal matter."

"I did. Better if I explain in person. I can drive down to see you in Corvallis."

"Fine with me," said Lorenzo. "It's best if I stay in town while I'm getting things organized. Dinner?"

"Okay. Tonight?"

"Perfect. Do you know Big River? It's on First Street, on the Willamette, as you might have guessed. How about seven o'clock?"

"See you then."

As he hung up the phone, Lorenzo saw that an email had come in from Tom and sat down to read it.

> *Maxine March has always been pretty toxic for me. She's someone who when you help her, you wind up in worse shape than when you started out. That being said, I've never been able to turn her down. I don't know a lot about Tito. I saw him only once, a year or so ago. Maxine found him, alone and in the streets, when she was on assignment in Ecuador. My friend Paul Bickford brought him into the country for her. No papers. No nothing. Paul's an army spook who does a lot of stuff off the books. Do it now and figure it out later seems to be the way he operates. They were a couple and went off together to live happily ever after with this kid. That's all I know. Good luck, Lorenzo. And be careful. As I said, Maxine can be toxic.*

CHAPTER

BIG RIVER WAS IN ONE OF THOSE former industrial buildings where you see the heating and air conditioning ducts when you looked up at the ceiling. Part of the rejuvenation of this part of Corvallis after a park was developed along the Willamette River, it had an inviting atmosphere and great food. Its booths also offered great privacy. Lorenzo arrived first and asked for the last one in the room.

"I'm expecting someone, but I'll be able to spot him from here," he told the hostess, a young woman who was probably a university student. As he scanned the menu, a young Hispanic man filled the water glasses and set a plate of bread on the table.

"*Gracias, mi amigo,*" said Lorenzo.

"*Por nada, señor.*"

Thad Sampson walked in and spied Lorenzo before the hostess could react, and made a beeline to the booth. Lorenzo stood up and they embraced with a gentlemanly hug and pat on the back that belied their earlier intimacy.

"You look great, Renzo," Thad said, sitting down across the table. "Ageless as always. And I like your new look: not quite a beard, but not clean shaven either."

"It's more like I sometimes get tired of shaving," said Lorenzo, rubbing his face.

"Not sure about the ageless part, Thaddie. I'm feeling my age more and more each year, or hell, each day."

They talked for a bit about their careers and people they knew. A waiter came and took their wine and food orders.

"How'd things go for that guy you were trying to get into witness protection?" asked Thad.

"Perez? I'm not sure. People in that program simply vanish," said Lorenzo.

"Great thing for you to do, especially when he'd tried to kill you all those times."

"Yeah, I guess. I try to help people, whoever they are."

"But I gather those days are gone for now?"

"Yeah," said Lorenzo. "Being a saint doesn't pay the bills. I was going broke fast when I was doing only immigration law. Those people—my people—needed my help, but I have to admit I got really tired of handling only that kind of cases."

"So you've opened your own shop here," said Thad. "I think that's great. You've dealt with criminal and civil cases before, so that will be your focus again, I gather."

"That's it. Almost anything but divorce, bankruptcy, and probate."

"How do you feel about involuntary commitment with a political tinge?"

Lorenzo leaned forward. "I'm interested. Tell me more."

Just then the waiter arrived with their dinners—steak for Lorenzo, fish for Thad.

"Andy Corning was my roommate at Willamette," continued Thad. "Came from a wealthy Portland family. Old money, trust fund, that kind of thing. Andy was always a bit wild, experimenting with drugs and alcohol. Lots of girlfriends and many one-night stands, sometimes in our room. His father sent him to a lot of psychiatrists who put him on a lot of medication. Nothing seemed to work until he met Grace, another Willamette student who was a year older than we were. No trust funds for her. She was a scholarship student who had to work. But she maintained a 4.0 GPA all four years."

"So Grace turned him around?"

"Exactly. He started studying and boosted himself off probation and was soon getting a sprinkling of Bs among all of his Cs. They graduated, and she got into a management training program at Nike. He went to work as an intern in his father's lumber business."

"I assume they got married, but are not living happily ever after, if I get the drift of what you asked me about before—I mean the involuntary commitment question."

"You are quick, Renzo," said Sampson. "They did get married about ten years ago. Andy is now 34, Grace is 35. They have two kids and live in a big house in Eastmoreland. But his wife is not the problem."

"Okay. She's standing by him?" said Lorenzo.

"Yes. A year ago, Andy's father died. Although Andy is an only child, his father did not trust him to manage all the intricacies of his huge estate. Andy's generous trust fund would go on forever, but the control of the estate—including the timber company—was given to the father's second wife, who used to be his secretary."

"Ah hah!" declared Lorenzo. "An evil stepmother, maybe from a modest background, who likes her newly found wealth and position and does not want some stepson standing in her way."

"You got it! And did I mention the stepmother's nasty son, who was once a logger in the forests of said company?"

"Don't tell me," said Lorenzo. "He wants to run the company with his vast experience. Did he go to college and major in business or forestry?"

"No way," said Thad. "He learned the business from the ground up—no pun intended."

"But how can I possibly help?"

"I'm not finished, my friend. Last year, Andy decided to run for the Oregon legislature. He hired a staff and began the arduous process of getting ready to campaign."

"The evil stepmother and her son did not want that, I presume," said Lorenzo.

"You got it again. For some reason—maybe jealousy or just plain meanness or to ace him out of his share of the estate and/or sabotage his political career—they set out to stop him. Leaking information about his drug-ridden past. Paying prostitutes to say he slept with them and beat them up. Things you'd expect the Trump presidential campaign to do, but this is Oregon. Stuff like that doesn't happen here."

Lorenzo shook his head in disdain. "Yeah, like you said, this is Oregon."

"It hit Andy pretty hard and he dropped out of the senate race. Now he's pretty vulnerable on the best of days; got off his meds, became very depressed and agitated. There was an ugly scene at the timber company office with a lot of other people around, and Andy threatened both stepmother and stepbrother with a box cutter. They called, not the police, but a psychiatrist, who guided them to a friendly judge who got him committed to a private psychiatric clinic for six months. His political future, his marriage, his good health—all of it over in a flash."

"What can I do for him?" asked Lorenzo, shaking his head. "I've never handled anything like this before."

"You're smart. You'll figure it out," said Thad, signaling the waiter for the check. "Here's a number you can call to get into the clinic to see him. I've got to run."

As he stood up, Thad dropped an envelope on the table. Lorenzo opened it and found a check for $10,000 made out to him with the notation "Legal Retainer" in the lower left corner.

CHAPTER

4

EARLY THE NEXT MORNING, Lorenzo met Sam for breakfast at New Morning Bakery, a local restaurant with good coffee and countless pastries, muffins, and bagels to choose from.

"Your apartment is okay?" asked Lorenzo, as Sam slid into the booth opposite him. "And your car? It's running okay?"

"Yeah to both questions, boss. I like the apartment a lot. Seems like mostly graduate students live there, so it's nice and quiet. The car? Well, it looks like hell, but it runs good."

Sam gobbled down a chocolate chip muffin and large cinnamon roll as they talked, covering the table and the front of his shirt with crumbs.

"Good, good," Lorenzo said, dabbing his mouth with a napkin, then continuing to eat his bagel and sipping his coffee.

"Is this a demonstration about how to eat right?" asked Sam, smiling at Lorenzo with bits of food in his teeth. "I mean, without getting stuff all over my mouth? I know I'm messy, but I learned to eat in the ghetto. Don't forget that!"

Lorenzo smiled and finished his food. "Excuses, excuses. Get us more coffee, and I'll fill you in on what I want you to do today."

For the next half-hour, Lorenzo told

Sam the story of Andy Corning.

"Shee-it!" he said when Lorenzo had finished. "White people sure have problems Black people don't even think of. I mean, you'd think he'd be able to get along okay, with all that money and stuff."

"It's a cliché, but money doesn't always make you happy," said Lorenzo. "You'll figure that out when you have some."

Sam shrugged his shoulders. "I'm hope'n that day gets here sooner than later!"

"You never know. For now, let me tell you what I want you to do. Go to the law library at Willamette University and look up references on involuntary commitment in Oregon."

"Where? You forget, boss, I'm new to this state. Where in the hell is Willam-ut what?"

"Check out the Google map on your phone. It'll tell you where it is. It'll take you an hour or so to drive there. Once you're there, find the law school building." He handed Sam a slip of paper. "I've written down the name of a librarian at the law school. She's expecting you and will help you."

Sam smiled and took the paper. "I love it that you trust me on this, boss."

"Sam, you're my legal assistant. Of course I trust you, or I wouldn't have hired you and brought you here."

Sam smiled and drank the rest of his coffee.

Lorenzo continued. "What you're looking for is case law on involuntary commitment. Write down the dates of the statutes and details and anything you can find on specific court cases. I want a list so I—or you—can find out what legal precedence exists. Was this guy committed legally? If not, how can we get him out?"

Sam was furiously taking notes as Lorenzo spoke.

"Any questions?"

"Just one, but it's not about this case."

"Okay. What?"

"What's with the furry face? A new look for your rural clients?"

Lorenzo smiled and rubbed his face. "Maybe in part. But I do get

13

tired of shaving every day."

"Don't we all," said Sam. "I do it so people won't mistake me for a gang member."

"Back to business, Sam."

"Yes, sir. I'll see you this afternoon."

Lorenzo looked at his watch. "Time for me to go too. I've got a good-looking lady waiting for me."

"I thought you liked only good-looking guys," said Sam.

"That's for me to know and for you to find out, Sam," said Lorenzo as they walked out the door.

CHAPTER

LORENZO BUSIED HIMSELF WITH UNPACKING more boxes after he opened his office. Despite the mess around him, he had cleared off his desk to a presentable state. He heard the hall door open; Maxine March was on time.

"Hello," he shouted. "Come in, please."

March was attractive, of medium height with a trim figure. Her brown hair was pulled back, and she wore little makeup. Her nicest feature was her blue eyes, unmarred by any mascara. Her white blouse and black slacks were set off by a tailored green jacket. She wore an expensive-looking jade necklace.

"Great necklace," he said, motioning for her to sit in one of the chairs in front of his desk. Lorenzo sat in the chair next to hers. He usually avoided sitting behind his desk, because it created a barrier between him and the person who had come to him for legal help.

"Thanks for seeing me on such short notice," she said, fingering the necklace nervously. "I wasn't sure if . . ."

"I'd see you? You mean because of something Tom might have said?"

"Yeah, I guess so. He is still pretty angry at me. But what he's mad about took place years ago."

"I know, I know," he said, shaking his head. "But that's our Tom. Holds a grudge far too long. But why don't you tell me what you think I can do to help you? I'm going to take some notes."

"It's a pretty involved story, so I'll give you the short version for now."

"Please, feel free," said Lorenzo, resisting the temptation to glance at his watch. He poured some water and handed the glass to her.

"Several years ago, I received an assignment from *Smithsonian* magazine to do a photo essay called "Carnival Faces," about a form of entertainment all but abandoned: the traveling circus and carnival. I was aiming for geographic diversity in my photo subjects and needed a locale in the Pacific Northwest."

"Where Tom has lived and worked for years."

She nodded. "Exactly. After some hesitancy, he set me up with a carnival coming to the Taft area of Lincoln City, halfway up the Oregon coast."

"I've driven through it," said Lorenzo. "In fact, lots of times this summer when I worked on the coast."

Maxine sipped more water and continued. "Before I could take on that assignment, I agreed to do another one. You see, when you're a freelancer, you can't afford to turn anything down. I got the chance to fly to Ecuador to shoot photos for a big multinational corporation in London. The company had a number of projects going on there and wanted photos to illustrate their annual reports, company magazines, websites—the whole gamut of platforms you need these days to compete. No need for my skills as a photojournalist, I just needed to take shots of people and places and make them look beautiful. I'd try for unusual angles of things and portraits of interesting-looking people in a way that might humanize the big, impersonal corporation that was hiring me."

Lorenzo stood up. "I'm going to make us some coffee—just be a minute." He left the room, and she could hear him pouring water into a coffee maker and grinding beans.

When he returned he said, "We'll have some fresh brew in a few minutes. Please go on."

"The assignment went well, and I had accumulated some good images in a few days. The client was pleased, and I was getting ready to leave when I ran into a wonderful Spanish photojournalist I had met before. Inez Santiago-Verde was fearless and intrepid and willing to do anything to get images she could sell to media outlets all over the world. She had heard about illegal oil drilling by a Chinese company in a remote part of the Ecuadorian rain forest and wanted to get photos to prove it."

"That sounds very dangerous," said Lorenzo, his earlier boredom gone. "But you put aside your fears and went anyway?"

"Of course I did. We hired a small plane and flew to where we thought the operation was going on. We found it right away, and Inez started taking photos. At the same time, I noticed a man I had decided was from the CIA standing next to some Chinese men in what seemed like an advisory role. I had met him on the plane and later, when we met for drinks in Quito, he came on to me. After I turned him down, he seemed to be stalking me.

"Needless to say, when he saw us in the jungle, he realized we had discovered his secret—or the CIA's secret—and had to keep Inez from publishing those photos. When we got back to the plane, he was waiting for us with a bunch of thugs. They began shooting, and Inez was killed. I barely managed to escape. Then I called another friend of Tom's and mine."

"That would be the Army Special Ops guy, Paul Bickford."

"Yes. Paul. I should tell you that he and I have a past." She paused to drink some coffee, which Lorenzo had poured.

"Tom said Bickford broke up the two of you."

"Wishful thinking on Tom's part," she sighed. "He and I have never been on the same wavelength."

Lorenzo was interested in hearing her story but kept thinking of all he had to do around the office.

Maxine went on. "I am sure I'm boring you, but I'll get to the reason I need your help now. Paul rescued me from a small Ecuadorian village, inland from where I had been staying. The bad guys had found us and killed my army escort, who had introduced me to this great little boy—who also helped me get out of there."

"And that would be Tito."

"Yes, my brave little boy. Although I thought I had lost him forever, Paul managed to bring him to me here. He stepped off the plane with Paul, and he hasn't left my side since." She walked to the door and opened it. "Dora, would you bring my son in, please."

A grandmotherly looking woman stepped aside to reveal a small but handsome boy of about nine who was dressed in a suit and tie. He reminded Lorenzo of how he himself once looked.

"Tito, this is *Señor* Lorenzo Madrid. He is a very smart man who is going to help us."

Tito stepped forward and bowed slightly. "It is my real pleasure to greet you today, *señor.*"

Then he turned to Maxine, a startled look in his eyes, and said, "Mama! Mama! He looks just like me!"

CHAPTER

AFTER MAXINE ASKED DORA TO TAKE TITO DOWNSTAIRS to a nearby ice cream shop, she sat down across from Lorenzo, who had moved to sit behind his desk.

"Dora is a retired army officer who Paul pays to keep the boy safe," she said. "He travels all the time or I guess he would do this himself."

"He doesn't leave anything to chance," said Lorenzo, shaking his head. "Forgive me, but I have to ask. Are you and he . . . a . . . couple?"

"Not anymore," she said. "I guess I loved him once but not now. He is married to the army. But he loves the boy so we still have that in common. His job prevents him from doing much about this situation, at least publicly. His career would be over if the army found out he had smuggled a little boy into this country without papers of any kind."

Lorenzo nodded. "I can see that, but shouldn't he have thought about all of that before getting involved?"

Maxine nodded. "Sure. Of course he should have. But sometimes the heart takes precedence over the head."

Lorenzo risked being rude by looking at his watch.

"I'm sorry," she said. "I have rattled on too long. I'm sure you are busy, but I need to ask you something before I leave."

Lorenzo smiled. "Okay. Ask away."

"Will you represent me if the authorities

try to take Tito away from me and send him back to Ecuador? I have enough money to pay you whatever it takes." She pulled an envelope out of her purse and pushed it across the desk. "Here's a check for $5,000 as your retainer. As I understand it, that means I am hiring you, and everything we've discussed today is privileged information."

Lorenzo did not pick up the envelope. "That's only partly true. I have to agree to take your case first."

"Well, there is that, I guess," she said. "I thought that when you met Tito . . ."

"I'd be so charmed that I'd agree to take his case?"

She nodded, an embarrassed look on her face. "Yeah. I admit it."

"He is cute and deserving and in need of help," said Lorenzo. "We can both agree on that. But I'm not sure I can help him or you. Foreign adoption is tricky under any circumstances. But here you have possible political ramifications. Both the U.S. and Ecuadorian governments will probably take a dim view of how Tito got here."

"But Paul Bickford saved him from God-knows-what. He was living on the streets, for God's sake."

"Very true. But what's to prevent the Ecuadorians from considering this a kidnapping? And what's to prevent our government from throwing the book at Bickford for doing this? Tito could very well become a symbol of American overreach. Remember, Ecuador does not like us all that much right now. Hell, they have shielded that WikiLeaks guy from being extradited to the U.S. by granting him asylum in their London embassy. For years!"

Maxine March stood up and extended her hand. "I'll let you get back to work. Here's my cell phone number. Call me when you've thought it over. If you can't do this, I'll have to try something else."

The door to the hall opened and Tito peeked in, a big smile on his small face. "We had very good ice cream, mama," he said. "Dora sent me to see if you are ready to go."

March smiled down at him and turned to leave. Lorenzo stood up. Tito walked around behind Lorenzo's desk and looked up at him.

"It was very good to meet you, Tito," Lorenzo said, bending down.

"Maybe we will see each other again."

"It will be my pleasure if that happens, *Señor* Lorenzo. It is my strongest wish."

The small boy hugged the tall man and then followed his mother toward the door. In the doorway, he turned and waved.

Lorenzo sank into his chair and shook his head. "Why am I such a sucker for lost causes?" he muttered to himself.

Lorenzo spent the next few hours unpacking boxes and organizing his files. Try as he might, he could not get the thought of Tito's situation out of his head. Paul Bickford—and, indirectly, Maxine—had created these problems for the boy, but was not in a position to help much. As Maxine had said, admitting his role in Tito's departure from Ecuador would mean the end of his career and could compromise all the clandestine operations he was coordinating.

At 4:30, Sam Lincoln rushed through the door, carrying a jumble of files and several large books.

"This should be enough to get us started," he said, grinning.

Over dinner at a new Mexican restaurant downtown, Lorenzo filled Sam in on Maxine and Tito. They decided to talk about their other case in the morning, after Lorenzo had read Sam's notes.

"You going to take this case too, boss? Sounds like your kind of client. I mean, hopeless and stressed out with lots of barriers to victory," he said as they finished their meal.

"I like that phrase, 'barriers to victory'," Lorenzo said. "It fits my usual *modus operandi*."

"Say what?" said Sam. "Modus what?"

"The way I usually operate—going against the norm, I mean, doing things my way."

"Got it!" said Sam. "Just let me know what you want to do."

"We'll discuss it in the morning."

CHAPTER

AN EARLY MORNING CALL FROM THAD SAMPSON changed Lorenzo's plans for the day. Using his Justice Department connections, he had managed to get permission for Lorenzo to see Andy Corning at the clinic. Because it had to be before regular visiting hours, Lorenzo was up and dressed and on his way to Salem by 7 a.m. He called a sleepy Sam and told him to continue unpacking boxes and setting up the office.

The Oregon State Hospital had been immortalized years before in Ken Kesey's novel *One Flew Over the Cuckoo's Nest* and the subsequent movie starring Jack Nicholson. Kesey had observed the way patients were treated when he worked at the hospital. He put a lot of that detail into his book. Things were much better now. A new building had replaced the one in the movie, and investigations brought about improvements in treatment and living conditions.

The legislature had also authorized the construction of a private clinic on land next to the state hospital, the Cascade Clinic. There, patients who could afford it got more intensive treatment, private rooms, and a lower doctor/patient ratio.

Thad's assistant met Lorenzo in the parking lot with a letter authorizing his

admittance to the building where Corning was being held.

"Mr. Sampson said to wish you good luck," said the young woman. "He's sorry he can't be here to meet you himself."

"I'll bet he is," muttered Lorenzo.

"Pardon, sir?"

"Nothing. Thanks for bringing this to me . . ." He looked at the badge dangling from her neck. Unfortunately her name was obscured.

"Kelly, sir. I'm a law student at Willamette doing an internship in Mr. Sampson's office."

"Great. Thanks, Kelly. And good luck with your studies. You'll learn a lot from Thad . . . I mean Mr. Sampson. He's a good attorney."

They shook hands, and she walked back to her car.

Lorenzo turned toward the rather forbidding-looking building ahead of him. Although it was new, it still sent shivers down Lorenzo's spine, with its barred windows and dark gray façade.

He walked through the main door and into a small lobby with chairs lined up against the walls. Straight ahead a tall, muscular guard with unblinking eyes stood on the other side of a glass window. When Lorenzo reached the window, the man spoke to him using a microphone. His voice reverberated off the walls of the anteroom so loudly that it caused Lorenzo to jump.

"Boy, that's loud!"

"And you are?" asked the man.

"Lorenzo Madrid. I'm an attorney here to see my client." He held up the letter from Sampson next to the glass.

The man behind the glass barely glanced at it. "This ain't visiting hours. No one gets in to visit this early. The patients have their morning routines. You'll have to come back later." He turned his back on Lorenzo dismissively.

"Wait! You need to call someone. You need to get someone up here who will read this letter and let me in!"

The man turned around and walked back to the window. "I don't have to do nothin' I don't want to do. Rules is rules! I don't give a fuck who this letter is from! Rules is rules!"

"That should be 'rules are rules'."

"What did you say to me?"

"I was correcting your grammar," Lorenzo said, smiling. "An old habit of mine. You're never too old to learn . . ." He leaned in closer to the glass to read the man's name tag. " . . . Clarence."

"I told you to come back . . ."

"Problems, Clarence?" said a voice behind him.

A woman in an old-fashioned nurse's uniform walked up to the window and opened it. "Show me your paperwork," she said to Lorenzo, "and let me look in your briefcase." She put on her glasses and read the letter as Lorenzo opened his case for her to examine.

"Just my legal pad and a stray law book or two," he said, pointing into the opened case.

The woman turned to Clarence and motioned for him to open the locked door. It immediately opened with a buzz, and Lorenzo walked inside.

"Welcome, Mr. Madrid. I'm Sally Rizollo, head nurse on this ward. We got a call last night from the Justice Department that you would be coming in this morning. I guess Clarence here didn't get the word." She turned toward him. "Right, Clarence?"

The previously hostile man seemed cowed. "No, Miss Rizollo. I guess I didn't."

"We'll talk about it later, after your shift is over. Stop by my office, if you will."

"Yes, Miss Rizollo."

The nurse led Lorenzo to an elevator at the end of a short hall.

"Clarence is not our best employee," she said as they stepped into the elevator. "We don't pay our staff enough to attract top-flight people. He's been assigned the early shift so he won't have to make any decisions." She shook her head. "Like dealing with you and your letter. I'm afraid it threw him for a loop."

"That's fine," he replied. "I'm used to people trying to put up barriers between me and my clients. Lawyers aren't the most popular people these days."

24

"Like psychiatric nurses," she said, laughing. "A lot of our clients here think of me as Nurse Ratched, the fictional nurse in *Cuckoo's Nest*. I'm sure you know that story and that character. This isn't the same hospital, but I'm afraid people associate us with it."

"You're much too nice to be like her," Lorenzo replied with a smile.

They walked through two more sets of doors and into a small area facing more doors.

"Here we are," she said, opening another locked door by inserting a key card. She entered first, with him close behind as the door slammed. They were standing in a large room that, from Lorenzo's cursory glance, contained about twenty-five men and four orderlies.

"This is the Crisis Management Unit," she said. "These men have been found guilty of mainly violent crimes but are not yet committed to the hospital. They're being evaluated. We do some of the evaluations over here because the state hospital is understaffed."

"By violent, what do you mean?" asked Lorenzo nervously.

"Rape, murder, crimes like that," she said, in a matter of fact tone. "Don't worry, though, Mr. Madrid. They're all medicated."

"Why was Andy Corning put in here? I don't get it. He hasn't been convicted of anything! He's just sick!"

"Please keep your voice down, Mr. Madrid. That was not my decision. A judge ordered it."

"Sorry, of course it wasn't. I need to talk to him and then see if I can get him released, or at least transferred out of here. He could be in danger from these other men!"

"I doubt it," she said. "We've got pretty good control of everyone in here." She began walking across the room. "The conference room is over this way. For a reason I've never understood, the architects placed the conference room on the other side of this area, so you have to walk among the patients to get there." She motioned toward the rear of the long room.

"We're going to walk through here?" asked Lorenzo, a slightly agitated edge to his voice.

"Yes, I'm afraid so. It was the only place we could set up for you to talk to Mr. Corning on such short notice. We don't have many attorneys visiting the men in here."

As they started across what seemed to Lorenzo to be the size of a football field, a large, very obese man with only one eye suddenly stepped in to block their path.

"Aren't you a pretty one," he said, standing so close that Lorenzo could smell his bad breath. "I'd love to fuck you right now. I like brown men like you."

Nurse Rizollo turned and stepped between them. "Not today, Randy."

"I wasn't talking to you, bitch!" he hissed. "No one would want to fuck you!"

By this time a large crowd had surrounded them, and they began shouting, "FUCK NURSE RIZOLLO, FUCK NURSE RIZOLLO!" At this point the four orderlies advanced on the group, each carrying a can of what looked like Mace.

"Break it up, boys," said a young Black orderly in a gentle voice.

Several older patients stopped shouting and drifted back to the tables and chairs arrayed around the room.

"That's it, fellas," said an older white orderly with a goatee and pony tail. "Let's get back to your jigsaw puzzles. Have you seen that new one? It's going to wake up those cobwebs in your brains. It's a newspaper front page. Ever seen one of them? Real hard to match the pieces. You guys are so smart, though, you'll figure it out in no time."

More men drifted away, leaving only the hulking Randy and a small wiry guy who looked like he belonged in high school, not the state hospital.

"Do it, Randy!" yelled the small man. "Fuck this brown dude right here and now! You can do it, and I want to watch to pick up some pointers. I never fucked a man before. I need to see what it's like. This dude is real nice looking too. It'll be great, and I can watch. Okay if I watch, Randy?"

The big man grunted and another orderly grabbed the little guy around the waist and turned him around.

"Let me go, you shithead!" he shouted. "I want to watch. I need to watch!"

"You need a time out, Blake," said the orderly in a soft voice. "Let's go back to your table and relax a bit."

Blake went limp and the orderly picked him up and carried him to the other side of the room. In the meantime, Randy had turned his attention back to Lorenzo, who was getting more and more nervous at the scene unfolding around him. In only seconds, his presence had created a tense and dangerous situation.

"I like you, and I'm going to fuck you," shouted Randy, as he lunged toward Lorenzo and knocked him to the floor.

The room went black for Lorenzo as he felt the big man on top, crushing him.

CHAPTER

WHEN LORENZO WOKE UP SEVERAL SECONDS LATER, the man was moaning loudly as two orderlies dragged him away.

"Sit up slowly," said the nurse. "Lean against the table. Does it feel like anything is broken? Can you move your arms and legs? Your neck? How does it feel?"

Lorenzo moved his body slowly and started to stand up.

"Wait! Help him up and let him sit on that chair," she said to the orderlies.

As he got up, Lorenzo felt stiff all over. "I'm okay," he told her. "Just let me rest a minute." He looked up to see most of the other patients forming a semicircle around him.

"Okay guys," the nurse said, her voice raised. "Show's over. Go back to your activities. A half-hour until meds and then your group meetings. Move along!"

They shuffled off, many with pained looks on their faces. An older man stepped out of their way. He was wearing a suit and tie and bowler hat. He kept straightening his lapels and shifting the angle of his hat.

Then he stepped forward and, with a slight bow, put out his hand. "Delmar J. Evans at your service. My apologies for Randy. He is very loony most of the time.

He tried to kill me once in my room, but I fought him off with my cane." He raised a wooden cane with an ivory tip in the air. "Lord Jim kept him at bay."

"Another patient?" asked Lorenzo.

"No, indeed sir, that's the name of my cane. As noble as the character in that Joseph Conrad novel. Do you know it?"

"Yes, I read it in literature class in college."

"Okay Delmar," said Nurse Rizollo softly. "Time to get ready for your group meeting. You may want to read aloud to the others today. They'd like that."

The old man bowed slightly to both of them and turned to walk away.

"A real character," said Lorenzo.

"He's called the professor. Not sure he ever was one, but he knows about a lot of things and his orations seem to calm the others."

"Except Randy."

"Except Randy. I'm afraid the treatment is not working on him. Unless he is heavily medicated, he goes off like that a lot."

"Isn't he too dangerous to be allowed around the other patients?"

"I'm beginning to think so. He was pretty quiet for the first few months he's been here, but he's getting worse. You see, the docs on this ward are supposed to figure out if someone is really crazy or just faking it. If they decide that someone is faking, they are sentenced and go to prison."

"What is he in here for doing?"

"Let's see, he raped his own daughter and killed her boyfriend in a fit of jealousy."

"And that was not enough to lock him up for life?"

"He had a very good attorney who brought in a lot of experts to testify that the voices he heard made him do what he did. The judge was skeptical and did not buy into the whole argument. So he sent him here on a six-month hold. Lucky us."

"I think I want to see my client now and get out of here," Lorenzo said, abandoning all attempts at being polite.

"I don't blame you." she said. "Andy is waiting for you in the conference room."

Andy Corning was sitting in a chair by the window with his back to the door. He didn't move as Lorenzo approached. As he got closer, he saw that his client had been put in a straitjacket. He ran back to the door and called out to the departing nurse.

"Miss Rizollo, I insist that the straitjacket be taken off my client," he said. "There is nothing in the court order that requires a straitjacket. Please take it off!"

Nurse Rizollo followed him back into the room.

"It is for his protection and yours," she said dismissively. "We sometimes do it if we think a patient might do harm to himself or others."

"And why would he do that?" said Lorenzo, his voice rising. "He's trying to get out of here."

"Well, I guess I could . . ."

"Not *could* but *will*, nurse," he said. "Now!"

"Okay, okay. Hold your horses!"

The nurse walked over to Corning and began to unbuckle the many straps on the straitjacket. He barely moved.

"There!" she said, turning to Lorenzo, her eyes flashing. "Satisfied?"

"Look, Miss Rizollo, I'm sorry if I offended you. But my main purpose here is to help my client. That's what I came here to do."

"Okay. I get it. Apology accepted. Call if you need us." She walked out of the room carrying the straitjacket and slammed the door.

Corning stood up and began to rub his wrists and stretch his arms. "That thing's a killer for what it does to circulation," he said. "I'm Andy Corning, but I guess you know that already."

"Lorenzo Madrid."

They shook hands.

Corning was a handsome man—blond hair, no doubt styled by an expensive barber—with fine features and a glow about his face that bespoke of many years of careful skin care. Overall, he had the distinct look of someone who never had to worry about anything in his carefully choreographed life.

How different the two of us are, thought Lorenzo. Although he could match Corning in the good looks department, Lorenzo's background was very different.

Corning sat down at the table. "I'm really tired," he said, running his hands over his face. Up close, Lorenzo could see that his eyes were bloodshot and swollen. "God, Mr. Madrid, I have never been through anything like this in my life. I know I've led a privileged existence and been shielded from most of the unpleasantness in the world, so I never thought I'd wind up in a place like this. It is more awful than you could ever imagine."

"I've had my share of hard knocks too, but nothing as bad as this must seem to you," he said. "And, by the way, please call me Lorenzo."

Lorenzo pulled a yellow pad from his briefcase and a ballpoint pen from his jacket pocket. "I know what they said you did to get in here, but why don't you tell me what really happened?"

Lorenzo poured Corning some water, and he took a long drink before talking.

"My mother died when I was ten, so I was raised by a series of governesses. I'm an only child, and I didn't have many kids my own age to play with. We lived in one of those old houses in Dunthrope. Do you know it? Old money, on a bluff above the Willamette near Lake Oswego."

"I've heard of it," said Lorenzo. "A place where people who look like me only tend the yards and clean the houses."

Corning nodded, then continued. "I was spoiled and got everything I wanted. My father was gone a lot, and he tried to buy my affection by buying me things or, later, letting me buy things. Fancy cars, fancy clothes, fancy girls. I had it all. He bought my way into Willamette University. I didn't have the grades, but he made a big contribution to their endowment and I was in. Of course, I didn't think I needed to study, so I was on and off probation. I got drunk some nights and most weekends. Eventually I started taking drugs."

He drank more water and gazed out the window with a sad look on his face.

"I was a real mess. I knew it, but I couldn't or wouldn't do anything about it—until I met Grace. I knew from the start that she was the one, so I spent a lot of my time trying to prove my worth to her. I even started studying and passing my courses." He smiled at the memory. "Without her, I would probably be dead by now."

"Thad told me you went to work for Nike, then joined your father's lumber business."

"Yeah, that I did. I learned something about marketing at Nike and then was hired to do the same thing at our company, Corning Timber. Things were fine for a few years. My father seemed to value my work for the company, and we became close for the first time in my life. He liked Grace and loved the kids. We had him over for holidays. Did the whole family thing."

"And then it all changed," said Lorenzo, remembering what Thad had told him.

"That it did," said Corning. "My father met Annabella. Or rather, he hired Annabella Oglethorpe to be his executive secretary. She had held a similar position with one of Dad's old friends. He touted her qualifications and work ethic. She was also very British, with a cultured accent and haughty manner and all the rest of it."

"Your father liked what he saw."

"Oh, yeah. She also fussed over him constantly, ordering his clothes from a London tailor, arranging his trips, handling his personal business. Hell, she even started selecting the gifts he gave to my kids! Next thing we knew, she was going on those trips with him. And after they returned from Asia last year, they got married and she moved into the house. First thing she did there was to fire all of the household staff, people who had served our family for years."

"Of course, she had to remodel the house and hire her own servants," Lorenzo said.

"You better believe it!"

"And your father did not mind any of this? He didn't see what was happening?"

"Hell no! He loved it! You know the old saying, 'There's no fool like an old fool'? That applied to him, as far as I was concerned. Besides, his health was failing a bit. The strong and fearless business executive he had always been kind of vanished as he let her take the lead, even at the company."

"Thad said that her son entered the picture at some point."

"Oh, yes. Dear Peter. He was the product of a one-night stand she had had years before in Ireland. As soon as my father died, about a month after she took over things, Peter showed up. My father was barely in his grave when Peter appeared at the first board meeting of the company after my father's death."

"Out of nowhere?"

"Yes, out of nowhere. I had a seat on the board and expected to play a leading role in the company. Maybe not as president but at least someone in senior management. After more experience, I would take over the business."

"So, what happened at that meeting?"

"Annabella produced a notarized paper, a codicil to my father's will that named her president of Corning Timber and Peter as executive vice president and general manager. I—and the other board members—were astounded. This was the first time we'd heard of him!"

"I can see why," said Lorenzo.

"She sent around Peter's resume. He had worked for a timber company in Ireland, first as a logger and then a mill supervisor, but never as an executive of any kind. She adjourned the meeting soon after that. As she walked out of the room, she looked at me and said, 'More changes will be forthcoming'."

"So, what did you do?"

Corning looked at the floor. "I started drinking again. I learned that I wasn't strong enough to deal with this. Not her, not her son, and not this new upheaval in my life."

"From what Thad told me, things kind of went bad after that."

"Big time. I barged into her office one afternoon—my father's old office where I had visited him since I was a little boy. Things got heated pretty fast. I slapped her, and Peter came in to rescue his mother. I slugged him and grabbed a box cutter or letter opener—something sharp is all I can remember—and I went for his throat with it. By this time, someone had called security, and I was dragged into a conference room. Soon after that, two cops came in. They put me in handcuffs and that was that. I was screaming the whole time and crying like a baby."

Lorenzo held up his hand and poured Corning more water. "I think that's enough for today. You've been through a lot. You need to concentrate on getting well. And I need to concentrate on getting you out of here."

Corning looked at Lorenzo with red-rimmed eyes. "Does that mean you'll help me?"

"That's what it means," said Lorenzo, grabbing Corning's hand to shake it. "I'll be back in two days. I need to go over the court record and see what needs to be done. And, there'll be no more straitjackets."

"Thanks, Lorenzo. I feel a lot better already."

Lorenzo stood up and walked to the door. He could see the nurse through the small window, observing a white-coated man who was talking to several men sitting in a semicircle around him.

She walked to the door when she saw Lorenzo looking out. "Things go okay in here?" she asked, glancing at Corning, who had resumed his seat by the window.

"Things went very well. Can I ask you not to put the straitjacket back on my client?"

She looked at Corning again. "I think that can be arranged."

CHAPTER

9

AS LORENZO THOUGHT SHE WOULD, Maxine called him the following morning.

"Law offices of Lorenzo Madrid," said Sam, answering the phone from the other room. "Yes, Ms. March. I'll see if he is available."

Lorenzo smiled as Sam appeared in the doorway. "You make us sound big."

"We are big, boss. We just look small from a distance."

"Good morning, Ms. March," Lorenzo said cheerfully into the phone. "How are you today?"

"I've been better," she replied.

"What happened?"

"I can't talk on the phone. Can you see me as soon as possible? There's something I need to talk to you about."

"Let me check." He stepped toward the door. "Sam, what do I have later today that you can put off for me?"

"You don't understand," said Maxine, her voice cracking. "I need to see you right now!"

"It'll take you an hour or so to get here from Portland, so I guess . . ."

"I'm already in town," she interrupted him. "I got up early and drove here."

This woman is persistent, thought Lorenzo, and pretty pushy. He decided to push back a bit. He did have other things to do.

"Can it wait a few hours? I've got a pretty busy schedule today. You remember that I've just opened the doors here, and I'm setting up my practice. Let's say at . . ."

"I need to see you right now!" Her voice was sounding more and more agitated. "I'm downstairs. Can I come right up?"

"Yeah, sure, but I do wish you'd called first."

"I did call. That's what I'm doing now!"

The call ended before he could say anything more.

"Sam, better put the coffee on. Maxine March is on her way up." He had just sat down at his desk when he heard the door open.

"Hello, Ms. March," said Sam. "Who is this handsome guy?"

"This is my son, Tito. Can you watch him for a minute while I talk to Lorenzo? Tito, this is Sam, Mr. Madrid's friend."

She rushed into the room, seemingly in a panic.

"Sit down, Ms. March," Lorenzo said calmly. "You look like you haven't slept in days."

Sam entered with two cups of coffee in his hands. Tito hung back by the door, looking frightened.

"Good morning, Tito. How are you today?" asked Lorenzo.

"*Buenos días, Señor* Lorenzo," said Tito, bowing.

Maxine turned to the little boy and smiled. "Mama needs to have you stay with Sam for a minute while I talk to *Señor* Lorenzo. Can you do that for me?"

Sam walked over to the boy and swung him around before picking him up and holding him close. Both were giggling as they left the room.

"Sam's a nice kid," said Maxine as she sipped her coffee.

"The best," said Lorenzo, walking around his desk toward her. "Now, what's this all about?"

Maxine blew her nose and took another sip of coffee. "Wish this was something stronger," she said, shaking her head.

"I've got tequila," Lorenzo said, nodding toward a cupboard behind him. "No self-respecting Mexican is ever without tequila."

She shook her head. He stood still and waited.

"Where to begin?" she said. "Paul Bickford called me early yesterday to say that he is being investigated for what his bosses are calling 'human trafficking'."

"What? On what grounds? That's nuts. From what you and Tom have told me, there is no more upstanding citizen than Paul Bickford. Loyal. Patriotic. Dedicated to the army and his country."

"All true," she said, sniffling and blowing her nose.

Lorenzo handed her a box of tissues. "So, what happened?"

"He thinks that some other officers in Special Ops turned him in to his superiors. Actually one officer in particular. Someone he had known since he joined the army, someone he had always considered a friend. They were so close that Paul even told him about Tito and how he brought Tito into this country as a favor to me."

"Didn't others know about Tito and how Bickford brought him here?"

"Yes, but they are all enlisted men and very loyal to Paul, who had been their commander for a number of years. He is convinced that none of them would turn him in."

"But his old buddy was not so loyal?"

"Not at all," she said. "And it gets more complicated. His so-called friend—named Randy Briggs, by the way—has a wife who made a big play for Paul last year. After all, he is an attractive guy. When Paul spurned her, she got mad and talked her husband into turning Paul in."

"Sweet revenge," said Lorenzo, shaking his head.

They sat in silence for a few moments.

"I guess you want me to do something for Bickford, but I don't know anything about military justice. That's a whole other legal area. I'd probably do him more harm than good."

"No, nothing like that," she said. "I need to go to Ecuador now more than ever. If I can figure out how to adopt Tito, maybe that will help Paul. I owe him that. But it will also protect my little boy. I can't let them take him back there!"

"So you're going soon?" asked Lorenzo. "Well, good luck. Keep me posted, and let me know if I can do anything on this end."

She sat down and drank more coffee. "That's the main reason I'm here. I need you to do something for me while I'm gone. I mean, besides taking me on as a client. Dora quit yesterday. Just left me a note with no explanation. She's retired army so maybe someone threatened her with the loss of her pension. I don't know what happened, but she's gone."

She looked at Lorenzo with tears in her eyes.

"He's a good boy and eager to learn," she continued. "He hasn't been to school, but he is very smart. He especially likes science. I've told him about the sea and about lighthouses. He is eager to go to one. I love lighthouses, don't you?"

Maxine was babbling and not making much sense. The whole conversation was making Lorenzo very uncomfortable.

"You know Tom and I had our big breakup at the Yaquina Head Lighthouse. Paul Bickford was there too, and Tom said things that really hurt me. It was all very dramatic. It was raining hard and the wind was blowing a gale. We were shouting, and I knew right then that we had no future together. If there had ever been anything between Tom and me, it ended there."

Even though he was always worried about appearing to be rude, Lorenzo glanced at his watch.

"I know you want me to leave," she said, "but I have to ask you if you would take care of Tito while I'm gone. I was thinking that maybe you . . ." she gestured toward the outer office, "and Sam could . . . he and Tito get along so well."

Lorenzo stood up. "That's not anything I've prepared to do. I barely know you. I'm happy to help you with your case, but I'm an attorney, not a . . . a . . . babysitter!" Lorenzo realized he was raising his voice and getting agitated but he couldn't help it. "You are asking too much of me!"

"You okay, boss?" asked Sam from the door. "You sound upset."

"I *am* upset!" Lorenzo was shouting.

"Are you okay, mama?" said a little voice from behind Sam. It took a few seconds for Tito to peek into the room.

Maxine stood up and walked toward the little boy. "We'll be going now, sweet boy." She turned toward Lorenzo. "Thanks for listening."

Sam seemed to be sorting out the situation. "You mean you want Lorenzo and me to take care of Tito for a while? Shee-it, for sure," he said, nodding his head.

At that, Tito ran over to Sam and hugged him around the legs. "Thanks for being my friend, *Señor* Sam," he said.

Lorenzo sat down and sighed. He listened to the three of them chattering as they walked away. The outer door closed. His assistant did not reappear.

"Sam?" he said in a voice that could be heard down the hall and in the outer office. "Sam!"

CHAPTER

LORENZO SPENT THE NEXT FEW HOURS looking over the material on involuntary commitment that Sam had researched at the law library. Although there was a lot of material, he realized that he couldn't possibly manage in the highly competitive legal world without resources of his own. Photocopies of the pages of legal cases and court decisions made by a paralegal he had barely trained would not win the case.

It would take much more to prepare for the hearing when Andy Corning's stepmother and her son tried to block his release from the psychiatric clinic. Never one to second-guess himself, however, or doubt his ability, Lorenzo knew he would proceed and act as if he had all the resources in the world.

When Sam had not returned by noon, he began to worry a bit. He kept trying to reach Sam on his cell phone, but with no luck. However, as irreverent and cocky as he was, Sam was also dependable. So Lorenzo walked the block to New Morning Bakery and returned with tuna sandwiches and oatmeal cookies.

At two, Sam walked in the door acting like he had only been gone a few minutes.

"Where the hell have you been, Sam?"

The young man looked uncomfortable.

"Is your face turning red?" Lorenzo asked him.

"Boss, how the hell can a Black man's

face turn red?"

That broke the tension, and they both laughed.

Lorenzo dumped the remnants of his lunch into the wastebasket and pushed the other bag of food across his desk. He held out his coffee cup to Sam and said, "Fill this up and bring a cup for yourself. I brought you some lunch too."

Sam returned with the coffee and sat down in a chair across from Lorenzo. He slowly took several bites of food.

"You've got some tuna in your teeth," said Lorenzo, pointing to his own mouth.

"I'm not the neatest of eaters, boss."

"Okay, start talking," said Lorenzo. "You've stalled long enough."

Sam cleared his throat. "Well, boss, you see, it's this way." He paused as if building up the courage to tell Lorenzo whatever he needed to tell him. "We're going to be taking care of little Tito for a week or so." He stopped talking and looked at Lorenzo.

"WE'RE GOING TO BE DOING WHAT?" Lorenzo was shouting.

"Miss March was desperate and needed to head to Ecuador. She wants to arrange everything to adopt Tito. He's a really sweet kid who reminds me of myself at that age. Very smart and gets along well with adults and children." Sam stopped talking and caught his breath.

Lorenzo shook his head. "I can appreciate your kindness," he said ruefully. "But neither one of us knows how to take care of a little kid. Nor do I want to know. I am gay, Sam. I have loved other men but never a woman. And I don't have any desire to adopt a kid, like many gay people do. I may be selfish, but I like my single life and I don't want to share it with anyone, least of all a little kid who has a lot of needs. Shit, Sam! Why did you do this?"

Sam looked stricken at his boss's outburst but remained quiet.

Lorenzo began pacing. "Where's the kid now?"

"He's at my desk, looking at a book. I drove him around town, bought him some food, and then let him play in that neat fountain at the riverfront park. It's a nice place. Lots of moms hang out there with their kids."

Lorenzo sat down and stared into space for a while.

"Maxine March had no right to presume we would take care of Tito. Tom Martindale was right. She is one screwed-up woman. Maybe a bit *loco.*" He pointed to his head.

More staring into space.

"What did she say?" Lorenzo asked Sam.

"Something like she had to make the trip and knew we would take good care of Tito. She said she trusted us."

"Well, that's comforting. I mean that she wouldn't hand him off to someone she just met on the street."

Lorenzo stood up.

"Okay, here's what we're going to do. I have a guest room in my house, and he can sleep there for the time being. I'll buy him some clothes and see what he likes to eat. Then I'll try to find someone to watch him during the day. Maybe a retired teacher. I don't think we can risk sending him to school right now. Too many questions." He looked down at Sam. "And you're going to help me, Sam! You got us into this, and now we have no choice but to do it."

"Are you mad at Sam and me?" asked a little voice from the doorway. "I'm scared of people who get mad."

Lorenzo walked over to the little boy and picked him up. "Never, Tito. You and I are buddies."

"Is Sam my buddy too?"

"You better believe I am," said Sam, patting Tito on the back. "How do you say 'friend' in Spanish?"

"*Amigo.*"

"That's it, Tito," said Lorenzo, smiling. "We are *tres amigos.*"

CHAPTER

WHEN SHE SPOKE, Annabella Oglethorpe Corning sounded like she was well educated and refined. People with British accents often seem like they are from the upper classes, whether they are or not.

The reality of her life was far from that. She had grown up in a working class family in Liverpool. Her father was a drunk and her mother a saint, who did her best to provide for her children: two boys and four girls.

Annabella's intelligence and good looks propelled her out of that hard life when she was seventeen. The owner of a local clothing store saw her photo in the newspaper and asked her to appear in ads promoting holiday sales. It soon became quite clear that he had more than her modeling career on his mind. Without hesitation, she agreed to sleep with him if he agreed to pay her tuition for a modeling school in London. He agreed and also signed the lease for an apartment in London.

After she moved, Annabella continued to see him during his regular trips to London. He was coarse and vulgar and not very smart, but he was rich enough to buy her anything she wanted. She could stand to have sex with him if she closed her eyes and imagined he was young and handsome.

Her new life brought just such men into

her life for real. She was soon going out to dinner and the theater with good-looking men of her own age. And the sex was marvelous.

One night, in the middle of a particularly pleasant interlude in bed with Roger, a married advertising director she had gotten to know, Rufus, her Liverpool benefactor, arrived. Because she had had the locks on the apartment door changed, his key would not work.

"Annabella. Annabella." At first, he whispered her name. When she didn't answer, he raised his voice. "Annabella. Annabella."

From the bed, encased as she was in her lover's arms, she began to giggle.

"He's got it bad for you, old girl," Roger whispered.

"Don't call me that," she snarled. "I am not old, and I am no longer a girl."

"Just a figure of speech, love," he said softly, kissing her on the neck.

"ANNABELLA. ANNABELLA!" Rufus was now yelling.

"Can you get rid of him?" she asked Roger.

"Sure, love," he said, getting out of bed and putting on a bathrobe. Roger opened the door and said, "Whatta ya want, mate?"

"Who are you? I need to see my Annabella!" The man was obviously drunk. "Sheese my best girl."

"No one here by that name, mate. Now get on with ya, afore I call the coppers!"

From the bed, Annabella marveled at Roger's ability to use a Cockney accent so effortlessly. She heard the door slam, and he was soon taking off his robe and sliding into bed next to her. As she felt his body rubbing hers, she soon forgot the poor old sot who had helped her. Moaning in ecstasy, she thought about the next step in her climb out of a wretched life.

❦ ❦ ❦

Over the next twenty years, this climb took her into other beds, involving men with a lot more class than Roger was ever capable of achieving. The sex with him was great, but he was limited in how much he could help her. She slept her way to the top with a number of rich men—usually without her having to marry them. Each gave her expensive clothes, jewelry, and cars, and paid for trips to expensive resorts all over the world. In return, all she had to do was flatter them, accompany them to important events, and let them into her bed whenever it pleased her.

Along the way, she even had a son by one of them, an Irish aristocrat with a castle in the countryside, a mansion in Dublin, and a wife. Peter was not the brightest of boys and struggled through school, even with the help of the expensive tutors she hired.

After two years of clandestine meetings, she gave the Irishman an ultimatum: marry me or I'm leaving you. He chose the latter but set her up with a monthly check and money for the boy. She continued her life as before.

A one-night stand with an American timber executive led to a job offer in the United States. He wanted her to become his executive secretary and she agreed. With the proper work visa, she and Peter were able to move to America, to a state on the West Coast she had never heard of: Oregon.

Given her wit and guile and an unexpected head for business, she moved up the ranks of executives and became a board member and senior vice president.

Five years later her husband died, leaving her in charge of a very successful timber company. After she had maneuvered her stepson, Andy Corning, out of the way, Annabella was in complete charge and very satisfied with her hard-earned position in life.

🌿 🌿 🌿

Annabella was gazing out of her office window in a downtown Portland skyscraper when the door to her office opened.

"Some attorney visited Andy at the clinic yesterday," said Peter.

She turned around abruptly. "What do you mean, some attorney, darling boy? Who was he and why was he there? Don't we pay that head nurse enough to keep all visitors away?"

"We do, mama, but I guess she slipped up," Peter said sheepishly.

"Indeed she did. And so did you!" Her eyes flashed in anger. "I give you very few tasks to carry out and when I do, you screw up. Your father is a very smart man. An Irish nobleman from a distinguished family. Obviously, you did not inherit his intelligence!"

Peter hung his head. "I guess not, mama."

Annabella walked over to her son and slapped him hard across his face. "Get out of here," she said. "I don't want to see you anymore today."

She sighed and sat down behind her desk, then pulled a business card out of a drawer and punched a number into her phone.

A man with a gruff voice answered after one ring. "What?"

"Mr. Nick Conte. This is someone who needs your services. I pay every well, and I am very discrete."

"You sound pretty high-toned," he said. "Mebbe too rich for my blood."

"Having the money to afford your services has nothing to do with my status in life."

"Meet me in Washington Park outside the gift shop," he said. "Carry a rose. Three o'clock."

"How dramatic," she said. "I like drama."

"I'll bet you do."

CHAPTER

SOMETHING WOKE LORENZO UP early the next morning. He had slept alone for so long, the presence of another body in his bed was startling. As soon as he switched on the bedside light, he relaxed. Tito had snuggled up to him. The little boy moaned but did not wake up. Lorenzo lay there gazing at the kid, who did look a lot like he did at the same age.

At one point, Tito cried out but still did not wake up. For all he had experienced in his short life, it was no wonder he slept badly at times. Lorenzo got out of bed and pulled the blankets over Tito's thin shoulders.

At that moment, Lorenzo knew that he would take care of the boy for as long as he needed to. No matter that he had only met him a few days ago. Tito reminded him of himself at that age: a skinny, little brown kid who was easy to both ignore and push around. Lorenzo had helped people all of his working life, and he wasn't about to stop now.

Lorenzo realized that he was still sleepy, so he decided to lie down on the living room couch; he fell asleep immediately.

❦ ❦ ❦

"*Señor* Lorenzo," said a tiny voice next to his ear, "I'm hungry."

Lorenzo opened his eyes to find Tito staring directly at him. "*Buenos días, Señor* Tito."

"Mama says I need to learn English, and the best way to do that is to speak only it at all times."

Lorenzo smiled. "And what exactly would that IT be?"

"English, of course!" said Tito.

"Oh, is that so?" Lorenzo said, laughing. He sat up and began to tickle Tito. The little boy giggled and then fell to the floor in gales of laughter. They continued that for several more minutes, then Lorenzo stood up.

"Don't ever get old, Tito," Lorenzo groaned. "You get very creaky."

"Like the hinges on a door, *Señor* Lorenzo?"

"Like the hinges on a door."

Then Lorenzo made sounds like a squeaking door and raised his arms like some kind of monster. He chased the squealing Tito around the room until he caught him and picked him up.

"Okay. The fun is over. Do you know how to take a shower?"

The boy looked perplexed.

"How about a bath?"

"Oh yes, in a big tub."

"Good. Come into the bathroom, and I will fill the tub with water so you can get all cleaned up. Okay? Can you do it?"

"Yes, *Señor* Lorenzo. I will like doing that. Mama says everyone should be clean at all times."

"While you're doing that, I'll throw some clothes on and fix us something to eat."

As Lorenzo cooked the oatmeal and made the toast, he could hear the boy splashing around in the tub. Not a bad sound at all, he thought.

🌿 🌿 🌿

After breakfast, he and Tito drove downtown to his office. Tito ran ahead of him down the hall and opened the door so quickly that it slammed against the wall.

"Goddammit, little boss, you scared me," said Sam.

The boy ran to him and jumped into his outstretched arms. "*Señor* Sam, *Señor* Sam!" he shouted. "Are you my sitter of babies?"

Both Sam and Lorenzo laughed.

"It's called babysitter here in the States," explained Lorenzo. "But Sam is only going to do that temporarily."

Sam looked stricken.

Sensing his disappointment, Lorenzo quickly added, "Only for a little while. We're going to find someone who will watch you when I'm not with you and teach you the things little boys and girls need to know to get ahead in life."

"Like reading and writing?"

"You bet, and learning math."

"What is math?" asked the boy.

"Numbers," said Sam. "One plus one equals two."

The boy nodded and smiled.

"Can we play now, Sam, while *Señor* Lorenzo does work?" he said.

"Okay, Sam," Lorenzo said. "Forget the boxes and files for now. Take Tito down to the park and maybe the library. They've got a children's section, I'm sure. While you're gone, I'll try to find someone to be his teacher and babysitter. I promise that this will only be for a day or two. Okay, you two?"

"Sure boss, whatever you say," said Sam, reluctantly. "I will get my old job back, right?"

"Of course, and a raise too."

Sam smiled and turned to the boy, who was tugging on his hand.

"Sam is taking me around this town," Tito said to Lorenzo. "*Señor* Sam is my very good friend."

Lorenzo handed Sam some money and said, "Don't spend it all in one place. See you back here at noon."

After Sam and Tito had left, Lorenzo sat down at his desk to think about who he might find to help him. After a few fruitless calls, he punched in the number of a retired nanny who had worked overseas. She had moved to town three years ago to take care of her mother, who had since died. She had previously worked as a tutor for the children of a wealthy European couple for a while but was no longer working. She came with the high recommendation of the chairwoman of the

OSU child development department, who Lorenzo had met at a party a month before.

"Is this Josephine O'Brien?"

The voice that answered the phone was friendly but guarded. "Yes, that's me. And who might you be, sir?"

"Lorenzo Madrid."

"Like the city in Spain?"

"That is correct. I'm looking for a nanny."

"I used to work in Madrid for a family with two little kiddies. The boy was a little darling. But the girl? A holy terror."

Lorenzo laughed. "From the sound of your voice, I can only imagine the problems she caused you."

"You are so right, sir. Do you have boys or girls?"

"One boy."

"And what age is your son?"

Lorenzo paused to consider his answer. It was too complicated to explain Tito's situation over the phone. He'd do that later.

"Tito is nine."

"A lovely age. If the truth be told, I do like little boys best. Don't tell the mothers of little girls that I said that, please."

"Your secret is safe with me," said Lorenzo, who liked the way Miss O'Brien sounded. "Can you come to my office this afternoon and meet Tito? I really need someone to take care of him right away."

"Yes, I can make it today," she replied. "Tito is a lovely name. From Mexico?"

"Ecuador."

"I know it well. I managed a widower's household next door in Peru. Poor man, he lost his wife in a car accident and was left with four little ones."

Lorenzo gave her the address. "I'll see you at two."

"Indeed you will," Miss O'Brien replied.

CHAPTER

WITH HER TOURIST VISA, vacation-like attire, and the camera around her neck, Maxine March had no trouble getting through the immigration and customs checkpoint at the Quito airport. The officer on duty compared her face to the photo on her passport and quickly stamped the appropriate page.

"*Bienvenido, señorita,*" he said. "Welcome to Ecuador. I hope you enjoy your visit."

He waved her through the turnstile, and she followed the crowd toward the baggage claim area. Most were tourists like she was, except for a few well-dressed men and women in business suits and indigenous people in colorful native dress. She had liked this country on her brief visit a year before, but had left under difficult circumstances that prevented a relaxed and conventional departure. Paul Bickford had gotten her out on a military plane, hidden among weapons and supplies.

As preoccupied as she was in retrieving her one bag, Maxine didn't notice the two good-looking men wearing suits and dark glasses who walked up to the customs agent and pointed to the blinking computer screen. They flashed their badges, and the man nodded and brought Maxine's information and photo into view. They spoke to him again, and he reached over to press a button on a printer underneath the counter. They snatched the printed paper out of his hands and left.

The men walked out the main door of the terminal and got into a small car parked in a nearby tow-away zone. In five minutes, Maxine walked out the same door pulling a medium-sized bag on rollers. A young boy ran up to her, asked her something, and she nodded. The boy raised his arm, and a cab driver nearly ran into him as he cut off another cab and a bus to park right in front of her.

After the boy loaded the bag into the trunk of the cab, Maxine gave him a tip as he held the door for her. The cab driver had not gotten out of the vehicle. He leaned back to hear her instructions and, without looking behind him, sped off at a high rate of speed, black smoke billowing out of the exhaust pipe. Two people crossing in front of him had to leap to safety and another cab had to come to a screeching halt to avoid hitting him.

The two men waiting in the car that was parked in the tow-away zone pulled out into the flow of traffic and stayed several vehicles behind the speeding cab.

After over an hour of driving through heavy traffic, the cab pulled up to the portico of the Marriott Hotel. A uniformed doorman opened the door for Maxine and she got out, leaning down to pay the driver. The doorman put her bag on a large cart and pushed it behind her through the double doors.

The men in the other car pulled up in front of the hotel and, through the large windows, watched her cross the lobby to the front desk. After she signed in and presented her passport and credit card, the smiling desk clerk handed her a door key card and a slip of paper. Another bellman appeared and picked up her bag. He followed her, presumably, to the bank of elevators not visible from the street, and they disappeared from view.

In the car out front, the man in the passenger seat punched numbers into his cell phone and waited. He rattled off a terse sentence in Spanish and disconnected. He got out, pointed to his watch, and then walked into the lobby. He did not walk to the front desk, however, but headed for a group of large chairs flanking the fireplace. He sat down, pulled a book from his coat pocket, and began reading it. Periodically, he glanced at his watch.

Upstairs in her room, Maxine unpacked her bag and took a long, hot shower. As the water cascaded down her body, she thought of Tito. That she loved him with all her heart was unquestioned. That she would do all she could to protect him was equally certain. He was not safe in the U.S. under his current circumstances. He was illegal, and that status was going to catch up with both of them sooner or later. Had her impetuous journey here put him in more danger? That was the question.

She was pondering it during the dinner she ordered from room service and, later, when she fell into a deep sleep.

Downstairs in the lobby, the big chair by the fireplace was now empty. With the spacious room vacant, the man could no longer pretend to be waiting for someone. He shook his head, looked at his watch, and shrugged his shoulders. *"Mujeres!"* he said with another shrug.

The desk clerk looked up for a moment, then went back to his work and did not pay any more attention to the man.

CHAPTER

JOSEPHINE O'BRIEN LOOKED LIKE she had sounded on the phone. She was short and plump and wore her white hair pulled back in a bun. She could easily play the role of the kindly housekeeper on one of those British television series where loyal servants downstairs take care of the rich and spoiled aristocrats upstairs.

Lorenzo saw her shadow in the frosted glass of the door, so he opened it before she knocked.

"Good God in heaven," she said with a gasp. "You scared the living bejesus out of me!"

"Sorry, Miss O'Brien," he said. "I saw your reflection in the glass. Come in, please."

She followed his outstretched hand as he motioned for her to walk into his office.

"Take your coat? Coffee? Tea?"

"I would dearly love a spot of tea."

"Done," he said, walking to the sideboard where he kept the coffee and tea and a small hotplate.

"Want me to do that for you?" she said, half rising from her chair.

"No, thanks. I'm used to it. It probably won't live up to your Irish standards, but at least it's not from a bag. I've even got a pot!"

"Bless you, sir. I appreciate your knowin' the difference."

He finished brewing the tea and brought the teapot and a china cup to the small table next to her chair. He poured a cup of coffee for himself and sat down to face her across his desk.

"Here's my job history," she said, pushing a large manila envelope toward him across the desk. He opened it and read through the documents quickly. Her experience was extensive. Although a native of Ireland, she had cared for children all over the world, mostly those from British and American families who were rich to begin with or held corporate or government jobs.

"I am impressed," he said.

"Thank you, sir. I'm glad."

"I do have one question, though."

She seemed to tense up and took another sip of tea for fortification. "Yes, sir?"

"With your broad job experience and work around the world, how did you wind up in a medium-sized city in the middle of Oregon?"

"I guess it is a bit odd," she said, looking more relaxed. "But it's easy to answer, sir, and no big secret. I came here to take care of my sick mother. I did that for a year until she died, and now here I am, high and dry."

Lorenzo stood up and shook her hand. "Welcome to our world. I think you will like Tito. He's a real charmer. I haven't told you anything about his past, but I can fill you in as we go along. By the way, when you plan Tito's studies, put in a lot of science. He really likes it and is fascinated by the ocean. I plan to take him over to the coast soon, so maybe you can prepare him for that."

"I will do that, sir, indeed I will," she said.

Both of them turned toward the sound of the office door opening. Tito raced into the room and leaped into Lorenzo's arms.

"What a lovely little boy," she said, smiling. "And he looks just like his daddy."

CHAPTER

EVEN THOUGH MAXINE MARCH HAD ARRIVED in Ecuador looking like a tourist, she had changed into business attire the next morning for her visit to the *Ministerio de Inclusión Económica y Social.* The uniformed guards at the door touched the bills of their helmets as she walked into the building. Inside, she took off her coat and laid it and her purse on a conveyor belt so both could be scanned by the x-ray machine. She placed her cell phone and a notebook just behind the other items. A young woman in uniform motioned for her to walk through the metal detector, which she did, passport in hand. After she had retrieved all of these items, she walked over to the desk ahead that displayed a sign for information.

A pretty young woman looked up from her computer screen. *"Buenos días, señorita."*

"Do you speak English? My Spanish is pretty rusty. I took it in school but never kept up."

"Yes, ma'am. How may I serve you?"

Maxine cleared her throat as she often did when she was not telling the truth. Was she lying? Just shading the truth a bit to speed things along.

"I am interested in adopting one of your children. I mean, a child from Ecuador, not one of your own kids." She was confusing this woman with her rambling conversation. "Actually, I am trying to find out how to adopt—for a close friend, like a sister to me, really. She could not make the trip and I could." She paused. "And here I am." She spread out her arms.

A look of alarm crossed the young woman's face but then was quickly replaced with realization. "You wish to see someone who can tell you the procedures."

Maxine nodded and the woman reached for her phone. She talked for a moment, then disconnected.

"You are in luck," she said, smiling. "One of our best case workers, Mateo Salcedo, is available to see you at this moment. He will come out here now and escort you to his office."

"Muchas gracias."

"In the meantime, you may wait over there," she said, pointing to some sofas and chairs next to the windows.

Maxine had no sooner sat down than a handsome man who looked young enough to be her son approached her. He was short and a bit stout but had a youthful face.

"Señorita March, I am Mateo Salcedo at your service."

Maxine stood up and the two shook hands.

He motioned for her to follow him. "My office is this way."

They walked through a door and into a large room where people sat at desks, talking rapidly into their cell phones.

He stopped at a door to allow her to enter a small, but elegant-looking office before he did.

"Those are beautiful carvings," she said, admiring the art in his office. "And the photos of the tortoises on Galapagos are magnificent!"

"You have been to our most treasured spot?"

"No, I am afraid not," she said, shaking her head. "I wish I could say that I have."

"Some day you will return to our country and visit there," he said, motioning for her to sit in a chair in front of his desk.

When they were both settled, he got down to the business at hand. "How may I help you, *Señorita* March?"

Maxine took a deep breath and started telling Salcedo her fictitious story. "So you see, my friend Georgia and her husband Grant want to adopt a child, preferably a boy. They cannot have children of their own."

Salcedo was shaking his head, a sad look on his face. "I am very sorry to hear all of this," he said.

She paused in the telling of her story. She had probably rambled on long enough and needed to get to the point.

"I shouldn't take much more of your time, *Señor* Salcedo. What I want to know about are the procedures my friends need to follow to adopt an Ecuadorian child."

"Yes, yes, of course," he said, handing her a booklet, which he began to read from. "You don't have to be a resident of our country, but you must come here to finish the process. This usually takes six to eight weeks. Once an adoption decree is issued, one parent must stay here until the whole process is completed, usually one more week. All the documents they present, I mean a passport and the proper visa, must be authentic."

"Of course," said Maxine.

"Are your friend and her husband over twenty-five years of age?"

"Yes, they are in their late thirties or early forties."

"Much older than you," he said, smiling.

"Don't I wish!" she said and returned his smile.

"Income is important," he continued. "The adoptive parents must show that they can support a child."

"That will not be a problem," said Maxine. "Both are professionals with good jobs." She hated lying, but what choice did she have?

"That is all good news for your friends," he said. "Here it gets a bit bureaucratic. I think you might call it 'red tape'."

"I know it well from my own experiences."

"Because my country is a party to the Hague Adoption Convention, children from here must meet the requirements of the convention. What is meant by this is that my government must consider if the child might be better off adopted by parents in this country. Then, the United States must issue to this child what is called an immigrant visa."

Maxine was trying to follow what he was saying, but her head was filled with thoughts of how blatantly she and Paul Bickford had broken the law the year before by taking Tito out of this country.

"Your friends should contact what is called an Adoption Service Provider who is accredited to operate here. They will take them through the process. Without that kind of help, I am afraid they will have no hope of getting the child they want to adopt." He looked up from the paper and smiled. "I think I must be overwhelming you with all of this material, *señorita*. Forgive me."

"Not at all. This is what I need." She stood up. "I have taken too much of your time. Thank you."

He stood up and bowed, and then escorted her out the door of his office and into the larger room.

"*Buena suerte, señorita*," he said, with another bow. "I hope your friends will find a son to adopt and, if they do, that they all live in great happiness. Marta will show you to the door. *Adios.*"

An older woman got up from her desk and motioned for Maxine to follow her out of the larger room, through the security area, and out the front door. Preoccupied as she was in processing all the adoption information, Maxine again did not notice the two men in dark glasses who were walking into the building as she walked out of it, even when one of them jostled her arm and did not apologize.

She hailed a cab and was on her way back to the hotel as the two men pushed through the security gate, walked quickly across the large room, and barged into Salcedo's office. One stepped behind the desk and turned the computer monitor so he could see the screen. He typed in Maxine's name and pushed Salcedo in front of it, shouting at him.

Their voices were so loud that many people in the large room turned to look, but quickly went back to their work when the second man slammed the door and closed the blinds in Salcedo's office.

Marta could not hear what was being said, but she assumed the worst as she crossed herself and returned to her computer.

CHAPTER

16

ANDY CORNING HAD HAD A ROUGH TIME in the few days since he had met with Lorenzo. Even though he no longer had to wear any restraints, this place was still a hellhole. First, a man in a straitjacket being transported from the small facility to the big hospital nearby had spit on him as they passed each other in the corridor on the way to breakfast.

"Pretty boy faggot," he hissed and let fly with so much spittle that it ran down Andy's cheeks.

"Jesus Christ," Andy shouted to Nurse Rizollo, who happened to be standing nearby. "You run a real first class operation here. God!"

Then Randy, the big lunatic who had attacked Lorenzo, came after him one day just after lunch. "I need to fuck you, fer sure, and I want to do it today!" he shouted. "You would be so delicious!"

As the big man lunged for Corning, the attendants grabbed him and pulled him away.

"You are not behaving yourself, Randy," said Nurse Rizollo. "You know what happens when you are not a good boy. You go into the dark for a while."

"I don't give a fuck where you put me as long as I have this good piece of ass in there with me."

The nurse nodded to one of the

attendants who shoved a needle into the big man's hip. He slumped to the floor, and they dragged him away.

Andy Corning went to the pay phone and dialed Lorenzo's number. "You've got to get me out of here fast," he said to Lorenzo's voice mail. "You've got to get me out of here, or I really will be as crazy as my wonderful stepmother says I am!"

CHAPTER

AFTER ANDY CORNING'S FRANTIC PHONE CALL, Lorenzo decided that he had to increase his efforts to get him released from the psychiatric clinic. He saw no other choice but to confront Corning's tormentors on their own ground. So he drove to the main offices of Corning Timber in Portland and went in without making an appointment. First he called the office and merely asked if the president was in town, and then he disconnected.

Although Lorenzo knew he was good looking, he never flaunted that attribute in daily life—except when how he looked might get him what he wanted. Whether it be in court—where he could play up to the younger women or guys who appeared to be gay—or by charming secretaries to get in to see their bosses without an appointment, Lorenzo didn't hesitate to play what he called his "good looks card" when he needed to.

This was the case now as he walked into the reception room at Corning Timber. He had worn his best blue suit with a red tie and white shirt that contrasted nicely with his smooth brown skin.

The young, red-haired receptionist was on the phone when he approached her desk.

"Corning Timber, please hold." She

pressed a button and answered another line. She smiled at him and held up her hand, mouthing "Be with you soon."

"One moment while I connect you," she said into the phone. Back to the first line. "Mrs. Corning is in conference. I will put you through to her secretary."

Lorenzo stepped forward. "Good morning, *señorita*. And how are you this fine morning?"

The young girl began blushing. "I'm . . . I'm . . . really good," she sputtered.

"I am happy to hear that." What rubbish, Lorenzo thought to himself. I don't usually talk this way.

"How may I help you?" the young girl said, her voice soft and quivery.

"I hoped to see Mrs. Corning." He handed her his business card. "I'm Lorenzo Madrid." He bowed slightly. "And you are?"

"Ginger. Ginger Longwood."

"Your name matches the color of your hair," said Lorenzo.

More blushing. She cleared her throat. "Mrs. Corning said to say she's in conference." She leaned forward and lowered her voice. "But I don't think she is. She's probably talking to her son. They are always in some kind of huddle."

"I hope you can help me get in to see her," Lorenzo continued, his eyes suddenly sad looking. "Tell her—or her secretary—that I am the attorney representing her stepson Andy."

Ginger punched in a number, as Lorenzo stepped back. He could guess what she was saying but thought it best to be out of earshot while she said it. The young receptionist's voice took on a tone of urgency.

"He is standing right here. Wants to see Mrs. C. but has no appointment. I know the rules, but I figured you could at least ask her."

She turned toward Lorenzo and smiled.

"He's Andy's lawyer!" she replied on the phone.

Back to Lorenzo again. "She's checking Mrs. Corning's appointment book. She's a very busy woman."

"I'm sure she is," Lorenzo said, smiling. "Do you know Andy

Corning?"

Ginger looked around nervously before answering. "I was his secretary," she said, a sad look on her face. "He was—is—a great guy and a good boss. I think what happened to him was . . ."

"I'm happy to see you're making our guest feel at home," said an icy voice with a British accent from behind them.

Lorenzo turned to see a tall, attractive woman in her late fifties or early sixties standing in the doorway. She had obviously spent a lot of time and money trying to keep Father—or, in this case, Mother—Time away as long as possible. She was dressed in a gray suit and pale blue blouse set off by two strands of pearls. She stepped forward and extended a bejeweled hand.

"Mrs. Corning, I'm Lorenzo Madrid," he said, shaking her hand. "Thank you for seeing me."

"We'll talk in my conference room. It's through here."

As he followed Mrs. Corning, Lorenzo turned to Ginger and whispered, "I appreciate your help."

The conference room was located at the end of a long hall. The large windows offered a great view of downtown Portland.

"Please sit," she said. "Would you like coffee?"

"That would be wonderful."

Mrs. Corning pressed a button on her side of the table and a young woman stepped into the room from another door.

"Angela, please bring two cups of coffee and those croissants you very thoughtfully brought in today."

"Yes, ma'am."

Mrs. Corning turned to Lorenzo. "I'm not certain exactly why you have come here without an appointment, but since it involves my stepson, I think it best if I record our conversation today. Any objections to that, Mr. Madrid?"

"None whatsoever. And you can call me Lorenzo."

"And you can call me Mrs. Corning!"

At that point, Angela returned with the coffee and croissants, which she set down in front of her boss.

"Please ask Peter and Mr. Conte to join us," Mrs. Corning said to Angela. Then she filled two cups with coffee from a silver urn and passed one to Lorenzo, along with the pastry. "Cream and sugar?"

"No, black is fine, thank you. You have quite a view," he said, gesturing toward the windows.

"Indeed I do," she said, sipping from her cup. "However, I would think we should dispense with this exchange of pleasantries and have you tell me why you barged into my office without an appointment!"

So much for his charm and handsomeness paving the way, Lorenzo thought to himself.

"Your stepson, Andy Corning, has hired me, number one, to get him out of the psychiatric clinic you have so illegally had him committed to, and, number two, to help him regain control of this company, one that is rightfully his."

"You can't talk to my mama in that tone of voice," said someone behind Lorenzo. He turned to see a tall, muscular man advancing toward him with his fists up. A shorter man walking slightly behind the first one grabbed his arm to keep him from hitting Lorenzo.

"Peter, calm down," said Mrs. Corning. "Mr. Madrid is a gentleman. His words cannot hurt me."

Peter turned and walked to a seat at the table far away from where Lorenzo was sitting.

"As you can guess, this is my son, Peter, who sometimes lets his temper rule the caution I have tried to instill in him all his life—alas, without much effect, I fear," said Mrs. Corning. She turned to the shorter man who was still standing next to Lorenzo. "This is Mr. Nick Conte, my new chief of staff."

Lorenzo stood and shook Conte's hand.

"Counselor, my pleasure," said Conte.

Like Lorenzo, the man was good looking, but there was something about him that seemed sinister. His eyes were a penetrating green that seemed to look right through Lorenzo. He was dressed impeccably in a black suit and black shirt with a tie patterned in dice.

"You must like to gamble," said Lorenzo.

"Why do you say that?"

"Your tie. The dice."

"Oh yeah. An old girlfriend gave it to me because she said I liked to gamble with other people's lives."

"Enough of this idle chatter," said Mrs. Corning, haughtily. She was obviously not one to be ignored. "Sit down, Mr. Conte, while we listen to what Mr. Madrid has to say. Remember, I am recording our session here."

Lorenzo nodded and handed her a folder.

"And what is this, pray tell?" she asked, opening the folder.

"It is what is called a show cause order from a court higher than the one your judge works in. I plan to file it later today with the circuit court. It asks that you produce evidence as to why my client, Andy Corning—your stepson—is being held under duress in a private psychiatric clinic when he has never been diagnosed with psychological problems of any kind."

"He tried to kill me, buddy," said Peter.

"He held a knife to my throat!" shouted Mrs. Corning, standing up so abruptly that her pearls started swinging from side to side.

"So why not have him arrested," demanded Lorenzo, "if he was such a danger to you both?"

"I was only thinking of his welfare and the future of his children," she said, suddenly letting a tone of concern seep into her voice.

"So putting him away as you did, by claiming he was psychologically impaired, was the lesser of two evils. Is that what you thought?"

"Of course," she answered, still keeping up the pretense of concern. "In spite of what he has put me through, I care about him. And the children are my grandchildren."

"Step-grandchildren, if I'm not mistaken," said Lorenzo. "How long since you last saw them?"

"That is none of your business!" she retorted.

"I have to ask you one more thing before I leave," Lorenzo said. "Will you ask your judge to rescind his commitment order? I can promise that Andy will not harm you in any way. He simply wants what he thinks is due him: his reinstatement in the company, as a board member and officer. He will only fight you in the courts and in this boardroom. All out in the open and legal."

"I am afraid that that will not happen," Mrs. Corning said, fingering her pearls. "I must also object to your referring to the judge in this case as *my* judge. He was duly elected by the voters in this district."

"With heavy campaign contributions from you and your friends. I've seen the finance records, even those you sought to suppress, which means that I might be seeing you in court on an entirely different matter."

"GET OUT!" she screamed.

Both Conte and Peter stood up and walked toward Lorenzo, who put his arms up in mock surrender.

"I'm going, but I'll see you in court, Mrs. Corning," Lorenzo said, smirking. "It's an old phrase that's trite, but in this case it's also true."

Lorenzo strode from the room at a leisurely pace. When he reached the front desk, Ginger looked up from her telephone console and smiled at him.

"How did it go?"

"Not bad, not bad at all. Take care of yourself."

CHAPTER

18

EVEN THOUGH HER ORIGINAL IDEA of adopting Tito in the conventional way now seemed impossible, Maxine was determined to keep trying. In the middle of a sleepless night, she thought of another way to go.

She had found Tito over a year ago in Montecristi, a small town in the western part of the country, which was where many of the world's Panama hats were made. It was there that a man she knew only as Grogan, one of Paul Bickford's Special Ops sergeants, had taken her away from the bad guys who were after her. It was there that she had met Tito, just before her own rescue by Bickford. And it was there that she hoped to find people who might know about her son's family.

Dressing to look as much like a native Ecuadorian woman as she could—with a billowy and colorful skirt, white blouse, and wool coat topped off by a derby hat—she boarded a bus at 7 a.m. the next morning. The lobby had been empty of all but a few maids and room service waiters as she ducked out the side door and walked quickly up the hill to the bus station. She did not check out of the hotel and did not mention her plans to go sightseeing in the local area, in case anyone asked where she was.

The bus was crowded, but she easily found a seat near the back, next to a sweaty fat man on one side and, on the other, an old woman who prayed loudly and rubbed her rosary during the entire trip.

The countryside was interesting but not spectacularly beautiful. It had a high desert look: sandy soil with a lot of low-growing vegetation, broken here and there by scruffy-looking trees. A range of mountains was set far in the distance.

Maxine was fascinated by the faces of the people on the bus: the smooth, unwrinkled skin of young mothers with fresh-faced children; the harder-looking women who had once been as pretty, but now hid their advancing age with heavy makeup; and men of all descriptions, from teenagers trying to look older with their wispy mustaches and carefully cut hair to older men with real mustaches and bulbous noses, wearing suits that were now too small for them.

At some of the stops, men would get on and walk down the aisle, trying to sell various items to the mostly preoccupied travelers. In one case, it was some kind of television program guide. No takers. Another man was pushing vitamins. Three takers. A third had small plastic toys for sale. Five takers. The men would pass out their wares on the first walk through, then collect the item or the money to pay for the item on their way to the front. At the next stop, they would get off. The drivers nodded to them and did not try to stop them. This was all very fascinating to Maxine.

She spent much of her trip reading the magazine she had bought in the hotel and gazing out the window. She smiled and nodded to anyone who looked at her but tried not to say anything beyond the few words of Spanish she had learned from a night class.

"You speak English, I presume," said a well-dressed woman who had taken the seat beside her at the last stop.

"So much for blending in," said Maxine, laughing. "I guess my disguise is not working."

"Your clothes were made in Ecuador, but the fabric is much too expensive and the tailoring much too precise to have been done around here." She leaned closer. "These people are mostly indigenous Indians—peasants, really," she whispered. "And you are . . . an anthropologist from America? An adventurer looking for a husband? A spy?"

Maxine flinched at that last description but tried to hide her unease. "Hardly any of those things," she scoffed. "But they each sound like something I should be doing. I'm just a lonely spinster in search of excitement."

"I like that," the woman said. "Politely evasive. I was just curious because I seldom meet anyone from abroad when I come to Montecristi."

"You come here often?"

"Once a month. I'm a buyer of Panama hats for several high-end women's stores in Quito. This is where many of the hats are made, not in Panama."

"I remember that from when . . ." Maxine caught herself, ". . . when I read about it somewhere."

The woman pretended not to notice that Maxine had stopped herself. "When we get there, you'll see women making hats in, how you say it in English, every 'nook and cranny'. Do you know what that means?"

"Wherever they can find space?"

"That is exactly right—in stalls and sheds and tiny rooms," said the woman. She turned to look directly at Maxine. "I have been very impolite. My name is Margarita Acosta. Most people call me Margo."

They shook hands. Maxine hesitated for a few seconds before deciding to give her real name.

"Maxine March."

To Maxine's relief, Margo did not seem curious about her and started talking about herself. She was the widow of a wealthy diplomat who had died two years ago.

"I'm sorry for your loss," said Maxine.

"Oh, don't be," Margo said with a grim look on her face. "He had a heart attack in bed . . ." she paused for effect, ". . . with his male assistant. A shock to me, my dear, as you can well imagine."

Maxine was getting more than a bit uncomfortable with such personal information.

Margo went on. "I got this job to forget him and all his escapades. Raoul was not his first affair with another man."

Maxine decided that it was time to change the subject. "So, how do you work with these hat makers? Do they have a union or an agent? Surely you must not have to deal with each one separately."

"I'm afraid I do," Margo said and shook her head ruefully. "It takes a lot of time, but I have known most of these women for many years, and they trust me not to cheat them—and I don't. If you're interested, I can take you with me when I visit some of them."

"I would like that very much," said Maxine, realizing what a great cover that activity would provide for her search for Tito's family.

Margo pushed her seat back and put on black eyeshades. "We'll be there in about a half-hour, so I think I'll take a short nap."

"I'll do the same," Maxine said.

She closed her eyes, but her mind was thinking about what she would do once they arrived in Montecristi. She would search for Tito's relatives, if any existed. She would check public records for births. If she had to, she would go door-to-door. That could prove impossible, of course, because local authorities might get suspicious and contact their superiors in Quito. If she took it slowly, she would figure something out. She always did when she put her mind to it—whatever "it" was.

CHAPTER

THERE WAS NO BUS STATION IN MONTECRISTI. Vehicles just pulled into a large cemented area adjacent to the plaza. This was where she had first met Tito. He knew Grogan and had been there to greet him. They had checked into a nearby hotel for the night, and Tito had met them for breakfast the next morning. The men who were after her—a renegade CIA operative and his Chinese cohorts—had followed her here and tried to kill her in the market.

Bickford had arrived by helicopter and a gun battle had ensued, during which Grogan and the bad guys had been killed. Bickford rushed her to the aircraft and they flew out quickly, leaving a distraught Tito behind.

Maxine let Margo Acosta get off the bus first. She had been good company on the trip but was a bit too nosey. Maxine needed to do things in Montecristi that were best done alone and in secret. Besides, Margo might have connections to the government her husband had once been a part of, and a phone call to people in Quito might put an immediate end to her mission here.

She could see Margo talking to a young man in what looked like a chauffeur's uniform. He picked up her bags, and they both walked to a Mercedes parked at the edge of the plaza. By this time, Maxine had stepped off the bus. As she looked up, Margo turned and waved to her, holding a hand to her face as if it were a telephone. "I'll call you," she mouthed.

Maxine waved, picked up her own bag, and headed the two blocks to the hotel, which was small but elegant. There was a restaurant just off the lobby and even a bar, although Maxine did not plan to do any drinking.

"Buenas tardes, señorita," said the desk clerk, an older man who wore a suit and tie and a carnation in his lapel. "Have you stayed with us before?"

Maxine hesitated. Although she was using her own name here, and Grogan had registered them both before in his name, she thought it best to lie. People at the immigration ministry could be looking for her.

"No, I have not had the pleasure," she said finally. "You have a beautiful hotel, and I look forward to my stay here."

The man smiled and bowed slightly. "Alberto Salazar, at your service. I am the manager and part owner. My partner was on the same bus as you. Perhaps you met her. Margarita Acosta is her name."

"Yes, I did meet her. A very charming and elegant lady. She mentioned her work with the Panama hat makers but said nothing about owning this hotel."

"She is my silent partner," he said. "She is more of an investor than an active part of the day-to-day things here."

"I hope to see her again," said Maxine. "I'm looking forward to my time here. Oh, I guess I said that already." Suddenly, Maxine felt an immediate need to get out of the lobby and to her room.

"We are so glad to have you. We will try not to disappoint you. May I see your passport and credit card, please?"

Maxine pulled the passport from her purse. "Here you are, but I'll be paying cash for my room."

Salazar looked surprised.

"I have just had an identity theft problem," she explained.

He looked puzzled.

"Someone took my wallet and started pretending to be me. It was a real mess, and I decided to use cash on this trip. I hope it will be sorted out when I get home."

Maxine took the tiny cage-type elevator to the second floor and walked to her room, which was spacious and clean. The furniture looked antique, but the bathroom had been modernized. The windows overlooked the street, and French doors opened onto a small balcony. Maxine felt safe in this room. She would be comfortable here for as long as she had to stay in town.

As she unpacked and set up her laptop on the small desk, she thought about how to proceed in her search for information about Tito. Several things worried her. Would her presence in Ecuador reignite any old investigations about what had happened the year before, and had anyone reported Tito missing? It was so like Paul Bickford to act fast and then leave others to pick up the pieces. She worried that she could become one of those pieces. And a new worry had just occurred to her: was Margo Acosta who she said she was or an undercover agent who would report her whereabouts?

CHAPTER

TITO AND JOSEPHINE O'BRIEN LIKED EACH OTHER from their first meeting. She started calling him "darlin' boy" and he called her "Miss Jo." Lorenzo and Josephine had decided that the boy needed at least six months of home schooling. His English was fairly good for a nine-year-old, but he needed more work. The multitalented woman had once been an elementary school teacher and was well-versed in history, science, and math. They began working together at Lorenzo's house. She would arrive at 8:00 a.m. and stay with Tito until Lorenzo got home at 5:00. She was available at night too. ("I have no other life," she had said. "Me neither," Lorenzo had answered.)

This was a prelude to Lorenzo's other plan for Tito's education.

Their real school would be in a small room Lorenzo had rented next to his office, so that he and Sam could watch over Tito, but still do their work. Lorenzo and Jo—she seemed most comfortable with that name—bought desks, chairs, bookcases, and a table for doing science experiments and board games. It turned out that Tito loved working jigsaw puzzles and was very good at it. Lorenzo had a white board installed along one wall, plus one of those old pull-down maps of the world and one of Oregon. Tito needed to know where he was living.

They named it "Tito's School" and Sam had a sign made to hang over the door.

They had kept these plans from the boy until they were ready for what Sam called the Grand Opening.

Three days after Lorenzo hired Josephine O'Brien, the magical day arrived. Sam bought doughnuts and milk on the way to the office. Lorenzo made coffee, and they sat waiting for Tito and Jo to arrive.

Precisely at nine, they heard Tito's voice from out in the hall. The door opened, and he raced to Lorenzo, jumping up in his arms.

"Lorenzo," he said with a big smile. "I did not think I would see you so soon this day."

"Hello, my good pal. Jo brought you here because we have a big surprise for you."

The boy's eyes got big. "A surprise for me?"

Lorenzo stood up and gently lowered Tito to the floor. He took his hand and led him into the hall, with Jo and Sam following close behind.

When they reached the door, Sam stepped forward. "Shall I do the honors?"

"Yes, do it, laddie boy," said Jo.

Sam opened the door with a flourish. "Here you go, my man. And don't forget to catch that sign," he said, pointing up.

Tito's eyes sparkled as he walked into the room.

"This is your school, my little darlin'," said Jo proudly. "It's a school for you to learn lots of things. You and I will learn together."

The boy raced around the room, hugging his teacher first, then Sam. He stopped in front of Lorenzo, who bent down to be on the same level.

"*Mi papa, mi papa.* I love you so much. *Muchas gracias.*" The boy kissed Lorenzo and hugged him for a long time.

"You are welcome, *mi amigo.*"

The three adults were all teary-eyed by this time, and Lorenzo wondered how he would ever live his life without this little boy at his side.

"Who wants doughnuts and milk?" shouted Sam.

"We do!" answered all three of them.

"So let's eat."

And they did.

Across the street, a well-dressed man put down his binoculars and punched a number into his cell phone.

"It's me. I'm near his office. I think I've found his vulnerable spot. We'll talk about it when I get back to the office. I don't think you'll have any trouble with him after I do what I'm planning to do. It'll take some time, but it'll happen. However, I think I'm going to need more money. These things are complicated. We'll talk later."

He ended the call and walked to a car parked nearby. He was smiling as he put a CD of an Italian opera into the player and sped away.

CHAPTER

MAXINE GOT UP EARLY and had a good breakfast in the hotel dining room. She was the only guest in the room when she went in. She glanced over the guidebook about the city but was really concentrating on her surroundings. Were any of the men or women who gradually walked into the dining room who they seemed to be or were they government agents looking for her?

As she finished her meal and gulped down the last of the coffee in her cup, she decided that such thoughts were ridiculous. Why would anyone be sent all this way to keep track of her?

"Ridiculous!" she muttered, as she sorted her money to pay the bill. She handed it to the waiter, who had rushed over when he heard her speak.

"Señorita?" he said, pulling out her chair. "You said something to me?"

"No, just talking to myself," she said, smiling at him. "Thank you for your good service."

"My complete pleasure. Juan Perez at your, how do you say it, disposal?"

"That is correct. I will see you at dinner."

She walked out through the lobby and into the street, carrying a shopping bag and putting on a large hat with a floppy brim and large sunglasses. Given her need

to fit in and the expectation that every foreign woman in town came here to buy a Panama hat, she had decided the night before to do just that. The search would also allow her to talk to people about Tito.

Merchants were just setting up their stalls in the town square as she walked out of the side street, so she decided to wait a while before checking them out. To pass the time, Maxine entered the nearby small, but impressive Catholic church through its beautifully carved doors.

As she expected, it was cold inside. It was, after all, April, which was fall here in the Southern Hemisphere. She zipped up her jacket and walked into the sanctuary. Wafts of various fragrances used in the services drifted her way. As she walked down the center aisle, the click of her shoes on the polished tile floor broke the silence. She was drawn toward the altar and the beautiful stained-glass windows in the wall behind it, so she sat in a pew to contemplate the restful scene.

At that moment, a priest walked in from behind the altar and, after genuflecting and crossing himself, began to place pieces of paper on the row of chairs to the left. Probably music for the choir, Maxine thought to herself.

She shifted in her seat and the pew squeaked.

The priest turned. *"Hola, cómo está? Español?"* he asked, walking toward her with a smile on his face.

"No, *Ingles,"* she said, standing up to face him.

"That's okay," he said. "We don't get too many Americans here except on Sundays in tourist season. Father Castillo. How can I help you?"

Maxine paused before answering, then decided the priest might know something about Tito, and she had to trust someone. She pulled a photo of Tito out of her shopping bag and handed it to him, asking, "Do you know this boy?"

He looked carefully at the photo, then handed it back to her. "There was a boy who lived here for a few years with his *abuela*—how you say, grandmother. He used to run all over town, never getting into trouble but always popping up here and there. I don't think he ever went to school, and he and his *abuela* did not come to church. She was an indigenous person, an Indian, and may not have spoken Spanish. The boy learned Spanish on his own and some English, as I recall. He was always tagging along with tourists to help them find the right Panama hat to buy. He seemed to be very intelligent and picked up the language easily."

"Do you have any idea where he might have lived?"

The priest's face seemed to change as he narrowed his eyes. "Why do you ask?" he said. "It is very unusual for an American woman to be looking for a little boy in a small town in Ecuador."

Maxine hesitated again and decided to shade the truth a bit. "A close friend of mine—a man—was in this town last year on business and met the boy. Over the course of several days, he grew very fond of the boy and decided to try to adopt him. He put off the application, but now he has asked me to pursue it for him—first, by finding the boy, and second, by filing the necessary papers to adopt him."

Father Castillo thought for a moment before replying. "We can go around to the various hat makers and ask them. Do you have more copies of this photo?"

Maxine pulled out more copies.

"I can pass them out to people who come to services here at the church," he said. "You might talk to the ladies in the market stalls. They don't talk all that much, but they see a lot."

Maxine shook his hand and said, "You have been very helpful to me, Father. Thank you very much."

As she walked out of the church and toward the market, a teenage boy suddenly appeared at her side. She ignored him at first.

"*Señorita, señorita,*" he said. "May I assist you? My name is Carlos, and I am at your service." Like Tito, he had a great smile. He bowed slightly.

"Do you know this boy?" she asked and handed Carlos the photo of Tito.

He studied it carefully. "Maybe, maybe not."

Maxine pulled a five-dollar bill from her pocket and handed it to him.

Carlos studied the photo again, then said, "Yes, I remember him from maybe last year or longer. He lived with his *abuela* in a little shack up that street. You want me to take you there?"

"Yes, please."

Carlos smiled again and took her hand. "Just follow me, *señorita*," he smiled. "I will take you there."

They walked quickly across the plaza and into a street to the left of the church. It was lined with small shops, many displaying Panama hats on racks out front, as well as toys made of the same material. They could see women inside, who were engrossed in weaving their wares.

Carlos led Maxine to a point a block or so away, where the shop buildings ended and many small shacks lined the now dirt streets. He stopped in front of one that looked abandoned and pointed.

"It was here that the boy in your picture lived with his *abuela*. I will help you go in if . . ." He looked expectantly at her shopping bag.

"If I pay you more money," she said, frowning.

"A boy has to make a living here," he said, matter-of-factly. "I have no schooling, but I do not sell my body as some do."

Maxine pulled another five-dollar bill from her pocket and handed it to him.

Carlos stepped aside and gestured for her to walk ahead of him, which she did. It was pitch-black inside, and the small room she entered smelled moldy and wet. She switched on the flashlight on her cell phone and proceeded cautiously. Then she tripped over a large object on the floor.

"Damn!" she said as she started to stand up. "Carlos, can you help me? I fell down."

No answer. Carlos, the opportunist, had vanished.

Maxine brushed off her clothes and shined the light on the object she had fallen over. The dead eyes of a very large rat stared lifelessly up at her.

"Jesus!" she yelled. "I hate rats!" But she was here, so she decided to go on.

She moved slowly into what seemed to be a bedroom. Two small beds were pushed up against the opposite walls, with an old red trunk set between them. Maxine lifted the lid carefully, dreading that she would find another dead rodent inside. Instead, a stack of letters, neatly held together with satin ribbon, and several photograph albums lay amid moth-eaten dresses and silk shawls. She shook the dust off the albums and opened the first one.

The photos on the first page made her gasp: Tito as a baby held by a beautiful young woman with a handsome man standing proudly behind them.

Suddenly a beam of light flashed at her. *"Ladrones!"* said a loud voice behind her. "Stop thief!"

CHAPTER

MAXINE QUICKLY TUCKED THE PHOTO ALBUM into her shopping bag. She raised her hands, turned, and walked slowly toward the flashlight beam and out of the shack. She blinked from the bright light as she stepped outside. The person who had shouted at her looked to be in his sixties. He was short and stocky and dressed in the brown uniform of a local police officer.

"No *Español*," she said.

He motioned for her to lower her arms and seemed to relax. *"Turista?"*

Maxine nodded.

"What were you doin' in this old shack? Nothing of value there. Were you lookin' for some kind of treasure?"

She pointed to her camera. "I am a photographer, and I specialize in taking photos of old buildings. This one is so old I thought it might give me some unusual views."

He held up his hands in disbelief. "Beauty in an old shack?" He pointed to his head. "Maybe a little *loco?*"

"Mucho loco," she laughed and pointed to her head. "Is it okay for me to go? I promise not to nose around here anymore."

He smiled and nodded. "Sure, you're free to go. I was only worried that you

would fall and leave here with a bad impression of our town. You like our little town?"

"Very much."

Maxine's first thought had been to ask the policeman about Tito and his grandmother, but she hesitated because her question might lead to more questions about why she was asking. And that might cause a report to be written and sent to Quito.

Instead, she asked if she could take his picture, and he readily agreed. He straightened his tie and repositioned his hat. By this time, a crowd had gathered, and they cheered at each click of her camera. When she had finished, she showed him the results and promised to send him a print.

Surrounded by children with their hands out for money, she started to walk back to the hotel. A familiar car pulled up. The chauffeur got out of the big Mercedes and walked around to open the rear door.

"Get in, my dear," said a familiar voice from inside. "It is time I showed you my home, and you look like you could use a cup of coffee."

CHAPTER

23

LORENZO HAD DECIDED that the best way to get Andy Corning released from his involuntary commitment in the psychiatric clinic was to get a friendly judge to intervene. At his friend Thad Sampson's suggestion, he had made an appointment with Circuit Court Judge Constance Browning the next day after getting Tito and Jo settled into their classroom. He left Sam with the seemingly endless task of organizing the office. ("I'll get it done, boss, you know I will," he had said.)

Thad had agreed to go with him to the judge's chambers since he had clerked for her soon after he got out of law school, and they were still good friends.

Lorenzo and Thad met in front of the Marion County Courthouse to talk about their meeting with the judge. The building looked like a prison to Lorenzo—the kind of Stalinesque archi-tecture that designers embraced in the 1950s and 1960s. Lorenzo much preferred the old courthouse buildings. Many, like the one in Benton County in Corvallis, had been built in the 1880s and to him evoked the dignity and sanctity of the law. Its renovation had preserved and modernized the old building.

"She is a fair person, but she can't—and won't—cut you any slack as far as the law is concerned," explained Thad. "I'm going along to pave the way for you, but I think I'll need to excuse myself after I introduce you."

"Of course," said Lorenzo. "I understand."

They took the elevator to the third floor and walked into the judge's outer office.

"Hello, Margaret," Thad said to the older lady at the reception desk. "How is my favorite person in the Marion County Courthouse?"

"Oh, Thad, you devil," she said, her face turning red. "We really miss you around here. I'll let the judge know you're here." She pressed a button on her phone and waited. "Mr. Sampson and Mr. Madrid are here . . . yes, I'll let them know." She turned to look at Thad. "She'll be just a minute."

"I'm being very rude," Thad said. "Margaret, this is my old buddy Lorenzo Madrid. He's also an attorney."

Then he gestured toward Lorenzo. "Lorenzo, I want you to meet my good friend Margaret Zuckerman. She kept me out of trouble the whole time I worked here."

Lorenzo bowed slightly and shook the woman's hand. "Good to meet you, Ms. Zuckerman. I'll bet he caused plenty of trouble for you to get him out of."

"Please call me Margaret. And no, he was always a good worker for the judge and very polite to all of us here." She looked closely at Lorenzo and back at Thad. "I think he has you beat in the looks department," she said, a sly smile on her face.

A buzzer sounded softly on Margaret's console.

"The judge is ready for you." She looked up at Thad. "When will I see pictures of your kids? I mean, your yet to be born kids. Thaddeus, you really need to get married."

Thad shrugged his shoulders and smiled at her. "Great to see you, dear Margaret."

As they walked toward the door, Thad leaned over to Lorenzo and whispered, "Why do so many older women think that every guy should be married? Why would I—or you—want to get married?"

"Beats me," said Lorenzo with a smile.

Thad knocked on the door, and they heard a muffled "Come in."

Judge Browning's office looked like a movie version of how a judge's chambers should look. Floor-to-ceiling bookshelves covered three of the walls. The other wall contained three large windows that overlooked the busy street below. All the furniture looked old and made of oak: the roll-top desk and chair, and a large conference table with six chairs arranged around it.

The judge stood up to greet them. "Thad. So good to see you. It's been a while. That legal conference on the coast last year?"

Judge Browning was tall and thin. She was wearing a white blouse and gray skirt, with a matching jacket slung over the back of her desk chair. Her black robe hung on an old-fashioned coat tree—also made of oak—that stood in the corner.

"Judge Browning, this is my good friend Lorenzo Madrid. We were in law school together."

The judge shook Lorenzo's hand and motioned for the two of them to sit at the conference table.

"I know your work, Mr. Madrid. I was thinking of that terrorism case of a few years ago. The cellist who was accused of blowing up a bridge, and you exposed FBI overzealousness to get her free?"

"Yes, judge. That was me."

"But you dropped out of sight after that. What have you been doing?"

Lorenzo hated talking about himself, but he knew in this instance that a short biography would be necessary.

"I opened a practice here in Salem, specializing primarily in immigration cases."

"Really vital now because of what is happening on the federal level," she said. "Off the record, I grieve for all those who get caught up in these ICE sweeps. These raids remind me of what the Nazis did to the Jews in the 1930s and 1940s. Horrible and so unnecessary! So many of the people rounded up today have done nothing illegal and have lived here for many years. But excuse me—sorry to get so carried away. Please go on."

"I got involved in a drug case and became a target of the leader of a cartel. I was kidnapped and almost killed. Two years ago, I closed my practice and moved to L.A. to teach immigration law at the UCLA School of Law. That was only for a semester, and then I handled legal aspects for a producer who was making a movie on the Oregon coast. That ended a few months ago, and I'm now in the process of setting up a practice in Corvallis." He looked at both the judge and Thad. "Enough about me," he said. "I'm sure I'm boring you."

"Not at all," said the judge. "I asked you. Knowing your background helps me evaluate the case I'm sure we will be talking about today."

Thad stood up. "I think that's my cue to leave the two of you to your business," he said. "I wanted to make the introductions and then get out of the way. Legally and ethically, I shouldn't know about this case or any potential case, for that matter."

Lorenzo stood and hugged his friend. "Thanks, Thad," he whispered. "I owe you big time, buddy."

"Judge. Always a pleasure to see you."

"Me too."

After Thad had left the room, the judge pulled out a pen and pushed a legal pad in front of her.

"Okay, counselor, tell me why you came to see me."

CHAPTER

WHEN MAXINE SAT DOWN on the soft leather seat of the Mercedes, it seemed as if she had entered another world. The chatter of the street vendors, the trash in the road, the decaying asphalt—it all vanished as the car sped along effortlessly, blocked out by the tinted windows.

Margo Acosta was dressed in an elegant yellow silk suit with matching blouse and shoes. She had draped a long silk scarf around her neck and fastened it in place with a diamond brooch.

"I hope you will forgive me for interfering back there," she said. "That particular officer can be tiresome at times."

"He thought I had broken in to steal something. I'm glad you came along. I think he was beginning to believe me but still had his doubts. I assume you know him and he knows you?"

"Precisely. He used to work as a security guard for my husband's property here in Montecristi. He wasn't all that good, but once we hire a person, we try to help them, even after they leave."

"I wondered," said Maxine. "He didn't seem to know very much about anything."

Margo nodded. "Petty crimes only, nothing important." Then she pulled a bottle out of a side compartment and popped the cork effortlessly. "Champagne, my dear?"

Before Maxine could answer, Margo

had filled two glasses and placed one on the walnut folding table between them. "How do the British say it? 'Cheers'?"

"Cheers it is," said Maxine, smiling. "Thank you."

The car rolled up to a tall iron gate. They had stopped at the foot of the hill on which Margo's Spanish-style house had been built. The driver stopped and spoke into the intercom.

"*Señora* Acosta."

The gates swung open, and the car drove through slowly, then through an archway and into a central courtyard. All four wings of the house surrounded the courtyard where well-kept grass and flower beds were set off by a three-tiered fountain bubbling water into a pool.

"This is beautiful," said Maxine. "What a wonderful place to live."

"I love it too, but my husband preferred the city—better to conceal his boyfriends."

A butler in full livery opened first Margo's door, then Maxine's door. "Madame," he said in a deep voice. "Please follow me."

Margo took Maxine by the arm, and they walked into the house.

The front hall was filled with Spanish-style colonial furniture and colorful Indian rugs strewn here and there on the polished tile floor.

"Edmund will take your things."

The butler obliged and disappeared into a side hall.

"Let's go into the drawing room," Margo said. She led Maxine down two steps into an equally elegant room with more antique Spanish furniture, paintings, and *objets d'art*, including a collection of Incan statues that looked like they belonged in a museum.

She motioned for Maxine to sit down on one of two sofas flanking a fireplace and walked over to an old-fashioned pull cord.

Edmund appeared in the doorway immediately. "Madame?"

"Coffee and some of those wonderful pastries Maria makes, please."

"Yes, Madame."

"It would be wonderful to have someone like Edmund," said Maxine.

Margo lowered her voice and said, "He is a gem, but I don't want him to get a swelled head. A gift from my late husband. He's from Argentina, and the people there are very elegant. He travels back and forth between this house and my city home in Quito."

They made small talk until Edmund reappeared, this time carrying a tray laden with a silver coffee urn and a plate heaped with pastries of all kinds.

"Thank you, Edmund," Margo said in an imperious voice. "That will be all for now." Then she turned to Maxine and said, "Tell me, my dear, why have you come to Montecristi? Really."

Maxine remained calm and took a sip of coffee and munched on a delicious croissant. Could she trust Margo enough to tell her the truth? Should she confide in her, in the hope that she could help her?

"This is getting a bit tiresome," said Margo suddenly, her eyes flashing. "I must insist that you tell me the truth!"

CHAPTER

25

LORENZO SHIFTED IN HIS CHAIR and pulled a file out of his briefcase.

"It's all here, but I will summarize the case for you now," he began, handing her the file. "My client is Andrew Corning, heir to the Corning Timber Corporation. He is the only child of the founder of the company, the late Edward Corning. His mother died when he was still a kid, so he was raised by nannies and tutors. Edward married his executive secretary, a woman named Annabella Oglethorpe, a few years before he died. As soon as they were married, she began to ease herself into the company, bringing along her son, Peter Trent, from a former liaison.

"Back to Andy, my client. He had been a typical rich kid—indifferent about his college courses at Willamette, drinking a lot and smoking dope, the whole rebellion thing. Then he met a girl who turned him around. They got married and had kids, and he expected to take over the company."

"Let me guess," said the judge, "the evil stepmother did something to ruin his plans."

"She did just that," replied Lorenzo. "He worked at the company, in every department, so he could learn all aspects of the business. He did well enough in these positions to please his father. Then his father died, just as Andy was becoming experienced enough to assume the presidency. At about

this time, Andy decided to run for a seat in the Oregon legislature. The main thrust of his campaign was to enact laws that would help workers in natural resource industry companies get higher wages and safer working conditions. His campaign slogan was 'From the forest to the ocean, Andy Corning is a man in motion'."

"Interesting," said the judge. "Corny, but it might work with some voters, I suppose. Let me guess what happened next. The stepmother did not want him to succeed in the company or beyond, like occupying a seat in the legislature. So what did she do?"

"Andy got very angry one day at all that was happening to him. He stormed into the office and threatened her and her son with a box cutter. The cops took him away and, long story short, she found a psychiatrist who exaggerated his condition, took the information to a friendly judge, and had him committed to that private clinic next to the Oregon State Hospital. That was a month ago."

"And you want me to get him released."

"Yes, ma'am, I do," said Lorenzo. "He is not a threat to himself or to society. Having him committed like she did makes a mockery of the justice system."

"Unofficially, I tend to agree with you, but I need to review the files and get another psychiatrist to interview Mr. Corning before I can make a final decision."

"I under . . ."

Just then, they heard shouts coming from the outer office.

"I demand to see this so-called judge!"

The door burst open and Annabella Oglethorpe Corning rushed into the room, trailed by the judge's secretary, a horrified look on her face, and a young man who hung back from the two women.

The judge stood up and walked toward Annabella. "WHAT IS THE MEANING OF THIS INTERRUPTION?" she shouted. "Tell me who you are and what you want before I call the police! I don't think you would like the accommodations in our jail!"

"I am Annabella Oglethorpe Corning," she said, in her best British accent. "I have reason to believe that you are discussing matters that pertain to me and my company. I needed to be present."

"Mrs. Corning—may I call you that without using your three names?" asked the judge. "You have no right to barge in here. I must ask you to leave right now."

"But you can't . . ."

"I can do anything I want in my court—or this office. I asked you to leave." She turned to her secretary. "Margaret, please show Mrs. Corning out."

Annabella squared her shoulders and looked directly at the judge. "You have not seen the last of me! Come on, Peter, we're getting out of this place!"

And they did just that, leaving both Judge Browning and Lorenzo with startled looks on their faces.

CHAPTER

MAXINE SIPPED HER COFFEE and took a bite of her croissant before answering Margo's question.

"I guess you leave me no choice," she said at last. "I'm looking for the family members of a little Ecuadorian boy I want to adopt. He is from Montecristi."

"So that's your secret!" exclaimed Margo. "I knew you were more than an empty-headed tourist! Is the boy here in Ecuador? In an orphanage? I have good connections at several in Quito. I know people in the ministry of . . ."

"Tito is not in Ecuador," said Maxine. "He is in the United States. He lives with me there and has for over a year."

Margo gasped. "You took him out of this country illegally? That is a very serious offense!"

"I know it is—or was. I didn't do this myself, but I was aware of it."

Margo shook her head in disbelief. "Please give me all the details," she said more calmly.

For the next hour, Maxine told Margo about her friend—not using Paul Bickford's name, of course—and how he rescued the boy and brought him to the U.S. and to her.

"Who was this man who helped you? A lover? A relative? Why would he do this

for you?"

Maxine hesitated. "We were once very close but are now only good friends."

"Why did he want to help the boy? A perfect stranger."

Maxine didn't answer for a moment, realizing that the truth would put Bickford—a man she once loved deeply and still cared about—in danger.

"He is a Special Operations officer, and he knew the boy through a man who worked for him." She paused. "Do you know what Special Operations is?"

"I know all about the Special Ops," Margo said. "In other words, he is a spy."

"I don't know what he does, really I don't," said Maxine. "And I don't want to know."

"But do go on with your story," said Margo. "It is fascinating."

"This other man, I believe his name was Grogan. I never got his full name. He helped Tito, I think. Bought him clothes and food and made sure he had a safe place to live. Tito's an orphan, you know."

Margo nodded her head. "So there was some kind of mission here, and that is how this man Grogan met the boy?"

"Actually, there was another man after me," said Maxine.

"Whatever for?"

"While I was on assignment in the jungle, I saw an illegal operation—Chinese workers starting to drill for oil on native lands. This other man was involved in it. He saw me and followed me here to Montecristi. I contacted my friend, and he rescued me, but Grogan was killed and Tito was left behind."

Margo sat there quietly, drinking her coffee and eating another pastry. "These are very good," she said. "My cook makes good pastries. Bad for the figure, but so good." She dabbed her mouth with a linen napkin.

"I don't know anything about his work," said Maxine, getting more and more uncomfortable. She had said too much already. This information was not hers to reveal.

"Go on, my dear," said Margo, her voice soft and reassuring. "I need to know everything, if you want me to help you."

"That is all I know." Maxine took a photo of Tito out of her shopping bag and handed it to Margo. "This is my darling Tito."

"He is cute and looks like he is very bright."

"He is very smart. Because of his uncertain status, I have not enrolled him in school, but I have hired tutors for him. He now speaks English easily and reads well."

"But this sword of Damocles has been hanging over your head," Margo said.

Maxine nodded and drank more coffee.

"Since he is in the U.S. with you, why did you risk coming here? This could turn out to be very dangerous for you. You know my government has not been very fond of your government in recent years."

"I know that, but I had to try. I went to the ministry yesterday and pretended that my husband and I wanted to adopt a baby."

"But you already have this little boy with you," said Margo, shaking her head.

"I couldn't reveal that to the man at the ministry. I just wanted to find out about the procedure."

"And you found . . ."

"That it is difficult but not impossible."

"Ecuadorian law has no provision for adopting a child by a single parent when the child is not present. You have no husband. You took the child out of this country without anyone's consent. I hate to use this word, but I must. You are a kidnapper!" said Margo.

"I realize that now," said Maxine, shaking her head sadly.

Margo stood up. "I am going to help you as much as I can and then see that you get out of this country safely and quickly. We can search for Tito's relatives together. Was that what you were doing when you were poking around in that old shack and I rescued you from that stupid policeman?"

"Yes. It was near where I last saw Tito. He had taken me there to find a Panama hat. Father Castillo suggested that I ask around and show his photograph to the merchants in the market. That led me to an older boy, who took me to the shack. I found some letters and old photos in a trunk, including one of Tito as a baby."

"What did you do with the letters and the photos?"

"I put the photos in my shopping bag, but the policeman came and you arrived before I had a chance to look at them."

Both Margo and Maxine looked up when Edmund appeared in the doorway.

"Yes, what is it?" said Margo, impatient at the interruption.

"Some men are outside asking to see you. They showed me their credentials. They are from the police. Not local, *señora*, but *federales*."

CHAPTER

"I AM ASTOUNDED AT HER AUDACITY," said Judge Browning. "She paid no attention to the fact that I am a judge or the legal ramifications of her outburst. I could hold her in contempt right now. I could call the security checkpoint and have her detained."

"Will you do that?" asked Lorenzo.

The judge thought for a minute. "Not yet," she said. "But I have to say that Mrs. Corning's appearance here in my chambers discredits her in my eyes—in effect, in the eyes of the court system I represent. Unofficially, Mr. Madrid, I would say that your case has been strengthened considerably. Leave your file with me to study, so I can think about this case and schedule a hearing soon, maybe next week. My clerk will call you."

"Thank you, Judge. I very much appreciate your consideration."

Lorenzo stood up and shook the judge's hand before leaving the room. He stopped by the clerk's office to make sure she had his contact information and left the building.

As he walked to his car, he felt pleased that his legal argument had worked and would probably lead to Andy Corning's discharge from the psychiatric clinic.

Until this moment, he had wondered if

he was up to the task of getting enough clients to build a successful law practice. The fame he had gained in his successful defense of the cellist in the terrorism case several years before had long since faded. The time he had spent running from the drug gang was wasted, as well as being very dangerous. His stint as a law professor at UCLA had been enjoyable but not very lucrative. The months he had spent as a movie producer were both fascinating and frustrating, and he had made a lot of money. But now, starting from scratch, a good outcome in this case would be very beneficial.

Before he drove away, Lorenzo called the clinic and left a message for Andy to call him as soon as he could. Patients were not allowed to have phones in their rooms, and he would have to use a public phone, so it might be a while before Lorenzo heard from him.

Lorenzo drove to a quaint "tea room" kind of restaurant near downtown that served good sandwiches and soups. It was noted for the many cakes displayed in glass cases. After he finished eating a tuna sandwich and tomato soup, Lorenzo walked up to one of the display cases to check them out. Everything from white to yellow to Dutch chocolate sat there, just waiting to be purchased.

"Somebody's birthday, I'll bet," said the friendly clerk. "Hard to pick one."

"You're right about that."

He finally decided on a three-layered dark chocolate, enough for his entire crew. He figured that Tito, Jo, and Sam would love it, and he wanted them to share in the celebration.

"Enjoy," said the clerk as she put the cake in a box and ran his credit card.

"Thanks," Lorenzo replied. "I know we will."

It was time to drive back to Corvallis to share his good news.

Since returning to live in Oregon, Lorenzo had been curious about the car ferries he had heard about. As was the case all over the country, in the past such ferries were needed to transport people and their vehicles across rivers. In Oregon's case, several ferries still plied the swift currents of the Willamette River, which flowed north through over half of the state until it emptied into the Columbia River in Portland.

The Buena Vista Ferry was the one on the route Lorenzo would need to take to return to Corvallis. He drove south on I-5 and exited the freeway near Jefferson. He checked the GPS in his car and saw that he could cross the river on the ferry, easily find 99W near Independence and Monmouth, and then head south to home.

He pulled up to the wide spot in the road where cars waited for the ferry to cross. The boat held six cars or two cars and one or two trucks, depending on their size.

The ferry came slowly across the river toward him and docked with only a slight bump into the two-sided slip. The captain gunned the engine until he had maneuvered the vessel into place. Only three cars drove off. Then a crewman used hand signals to motion Lorenzo forward. He was on the left, and two other cars drove on to his right.

The captain gunned the engine again, and Lorenzo could see in his rearview mirror that the crewman was beginning to pull up the barrier that stretched across the road.

Just then, everyone turned toward the loud, unmuffled sound of a large pickup moving very fast down the road. The crewman dropped the barrier, and the truck sped onto the ferry. Its weight caused the whole vessel to go down in the water. The driver, who was wearing very big and very dark sunglasses, revved the engine again and stopped only after it had touched the rear bumper of Lorenzo's car. He turned off the ignition.

Lorenzo, who was thinking about Tito and Maxine and how much he was enjoying the chance to relax, did not pay any attention when the driver started his truck again. Soon the engine was roaring, and the truck began to push Lorenzo's car with all the force such a huge vehicle could bring to bear.

Crewmen and people in the other cars were yelling and waving their arms. As Lorenzo finally realized what was happening, he attempted to unhook his seat belt. The driver in the truck kept moving his vehicle forward and had soon pushed Lorenzo's car so that it was teetering on the front edge of the ferry deck.

Lorenzo frantically pulled on his seat belt, but it was stuck and wouldn't release. The driver put his truck in reverse, which gave him more deck space to gain momentum. In a final push, he gunned the engine again, and Lorenzo gripped the steering wheel as his car dropped quickly into the river.

CHAPTER

"JUST STAY CALM, MY DEAR," said Margo. "I will handle this." She walked out of the room and disappeared down the hallway.

Maxine heard the front door open and then muffled voices. She stood up and walked over to a large window with a view of the driveway. A police car was parked there, the lights on the top flashing. Nearer to the door was a dark-colored sedan that looked like Margo's Mercedes. Five or six uniformed men were milling around the cars.

Suddenly, she felt faint and steadied herself against a nearby table.

The door to the room opened behind her. *"Señorita* Maxine Marsh?" said a voice.

Maxine turned to face a man in plain clothes. "It's March, not Marsh," she said. "But yes, I am Maxine March."

The man nodded and another man and a woman walked toward her. The man put handcuffs on her wrists, while the woman frisked her.

"You are under arrest for kidnapping a citizen of Ecuador and taking him to the United States," said the first man. "I must tell you that the penalties for such infractions can be very severe."

"I want to call my embassy," Maxine demanded, becoming really concerned for the first time.

As she was pushed out into the hall, Maxine saw Margo standing next to the door, a satisfied smile on her lips. She was holding the shopping bag containing the photos of Tito.

"How could you do this to me?" Maxine asked in shock. "I thought you were my friend!"

Margo scoffed. "An acquaintance, my dear, not a friend. I am also a patriot who stands up for my country."

"You used me. But why? This is a little boy we're talking about. An innocent little boy."

"You used the boy, why I do not know, but you used him."

"But he has done nothing wrong. I gave him a better life than he ever would have had in this godforsaken country."

Everyone stood still, and she could feel their hatred as they all stared at her.

Margo walked over to Maxine and spit in her face. "It is never a good idea to say bad things about a country when you are in that country, my dear."

As Maxine was trying to wipe the spittle off her face, Margo slapped her so hard she staggered backward.

The men led her to the police car, and Maxine heard Margo's voice from inside the house. "We will see how you like our prison system, my dear. Maybe you can write about that, since you will be getting an inside view!"

CHAPTER

BEFORE HE ENTERED UCLA, Lorenzo did not know how to swim. Pools were few and far between in the Boyle Heights section of Los Angeles where he grew up. But he took to the water easily and might have made the swim team, if he had been interested.

Now, as he felt his car plunging toward the bottom of the river, that skill kicked in as he tried desperately to escape. Luckily, he had opened the driver side window during his drive to enjoy the breeze, and the fact that his seat belt had come loose in the plunge made his exit from the car fairly easy. He held his breath and floated out of the car.

He figured he would be on the surface within seconds, until something stopped his ascent: his belt had caught on the outside mirror, and he couldn't move. He reached over to work it free, but it was still stuck. With his breath giving out, he finally managed to unhook the belt and rose quickly to the surface.

He was coughing so violently that he had trouble staying afloat on the fast-moving river. Just as he seemed on the verge of passing out, he heard voices above him.

"GRAB THE LINE! GRAB THE LINE!"

He looked up to see a man on the bank throwing a rope to him. Lorenzo reached for it but missed the first two attempts. He finally caught it and held on tightly. Within seconds, he was lying on the bank, still gasping for breath and coughing, but safe.

"You are one lucky son of a bitch," said the man, who Lorenzo recognized as the ferry boat captain.

"Thanks a lot," said Lorenzo. "You saved my life!"

Another man walked up to Lorenzo. The crewman.

"We called the rescue guys and the sheriff," he said. "They'll be here soon. Just stay calm."

"Help me sit up, please," said Lorenzo.

The two got on either side of Lorenzo and pulled him into an upright position so he could sit, leaning against a tree.

"Just stay put for now, until the ambulance gets here," said the captain. "You seem okay, but you never know. You might have internal injuries or a concussion."

"You're bleeding," said the crewman.

"Don't just stand there, Terry!" said the captain gruffly. "Get the first aid kit!"

After sitting there for a few more minutes, Lorenzo struggled to his feet. He could stand, but wobbled a bit when he tried to walk.

"Easy, big guy," said the captain. "You've had a real shock."

Just then, a sheriff's car pulled up and a lone deputy walked over. As soon as Lorenzo looked at him, he knew he might have a hard time. The man had "redneck" written all over him, both literally and figuratively.

The deputy's head was shaved and his face was red, like he'd been running. He strutted over to the three of them.

"Went for a little swim, Pancho?" he sneered. "Let me see your papers."

"Lorenzo Madrid, attorney at law. Let me see your credentials."

"Who's givin' the orders around here?"

"I asked to see your credentials. How do I know you are really a sheriff's deputy? You might be a rent-a-cop or something like that."

Lorenzo had faced off with Neanderthals like this before. He might be running a risk, but the guy made him very angry. This kind of thing happened all the time to the people he served, but they had no way to fight back. He did.

The deputy grew his gun. "Assume the position!"

The captain spoke up. "Troy, this man came close to drowning. He don't need any more . . ."

"Keep it to yourself, Justin. This ain't your fight."

Lorenzo did not move.

"GODDAMMIT!" shouted the deputy, "I SAID GET ON THE GROUND!" He cocked his gun and aimed it directly at Lorenzo.

"What the fuck are you doing, Troy?" said a voice behind them. Another uniformed man was walking hurriedly down the embankment. "Put the gun down! Go back to your car! Will someone please tell me what's going on?"

Lorenzo stepped forward and held out his hand. "Lorenzo Madrid, sheriff. I'm happy to meet you."

The sheriff quickly shook his hand. "Dan Masters."

Lorenzo started feeling dizzy and sat down.

The ferry captain motioned for the sheriff to walk with him along the embankment toward the boat, but Lorenzo could still hear them.

"This guy's in his car on the ferry when a huge pickup roars onto the boat just as we were casting off. He started rammin' this guy's car and kept it up until he pushed it off—with this guy inside!"

"Christ on a crutch!" said the sheriff. "What a stupid thing to do!"

The sheriff walked back over to Lorenzo. "Justin here was telling me what happened. Are you okay?"

"I think so, but I banged up my head, and I'm kind of dizzy," replied Lorenzo.

The sheriff turned to the captain. "Justin, did you call . . ."

At that moment a red rescue truck drove up and two medics got out, one carrying a bag and a neck brace and the other carrying what looked like a collapsible gurney. They ignored the other men and walked right to Lorenzo.

The first medic put the neck brace on Lorenzo and looked at the gash on his forehead, while the other one took his temperature and put a blood pressure cuff on his arm. "Everything is normal," he said to his partner.

"Are you in pain?" asked the first medic as he looked into Lorenzo's eyes with a penlight.

"No, just a little stiff," said Lorenzo. "I guess I'm lucky."

"Damn right, sir," said the second medic. "You are real lucky and in great shape. We're going to take you to the ER in Corvallis, just to make sure nothing is wrong. They'll look you over and maybe keep you overnight for observation."

Lorenzo knew the sheriff would want a statement from him about what had happened, but that could wait until tomorrow. Although he felt good enough to do it right then, he had the strong inclination to get away from there as fast as possible.

"I'm feeling pretty shaky, sheriff. Can you come by the hospital in Corvallis tomorrow? I'll tell you what little I know then."

The sheriff thought for a moment. "Sure, why not? I know where you'll be."

The medics helped Lorenzo walk to the ambulance, and he got into the back without assistance.

As the vehicle drove away, a short man stood watching from the bushes. He was dripping wet, and another, taller man handed him a towel.

"Better luck next time," he muttered to himself.

CHAPTER

30

AS THE POLICE CAR CAREENED DOWN THE HIGHWAY at high speed, Maxine kept murmuring to herself to "stay calm, stay calm." Even though she was not at all religious, she also closed her eyes and implored God to help her. She had been in some dangerous spots before—when you report from foreign countries, you always risk danger, everything from corrupt policemen and dishonest government officials to drug dealers and dangerous gangsters and even teenage gunmen hopped up on whatever narcotic is available—but never anything this bad.

Two thoughts kept coming to mind: contacting the embassy and, through people there, Paul Bickford. She also kept thinking of the case of another American woman she had once written an article about, who was accused of being a member of a revolutionary movement in Peru. She had been imprisoned for many years under terrible conditions in Yanamayo, a high-altitude prison where the cells lacked running water and there was no glass in the windows to keep out the cold mountain winds.

Would that be her fate? And how would anyone ever know that something had happened to her? She banged her handcuffs against the glass of the partition. "I DEMAND THAT YOU LET ME CALL

THE AMERICAN EMBASSY!" she shouted. "I HAVE A RIGHT TO CALL THE AMERICAN EMBASSY!"

CHAPTER

AT THE INSISTENCE OF THE DOCTOR ON DUTY in the Emergency Room at Good Samaritan Medical Center in Corvallis, Lorenzo agreed to be admitted for observation. After x-rays found no injuries to his arms, legs, and head, the doctor had him wheeled to another section where he was quickly assigned to a private room.

"You're sure lucky," the doctor said. "You're in great shape for . . ."

"An old guy," said Lorenzo, laughing.

"You in your forties?" asked the doctor.

"Almost fifty."

"I'm impressed. You take good care of yourself."

"We Mexicans are a hearty breed," said Lorenzo. "I guess I'm descended from peasants. You know, the guys pulling burros on a rope or sleeping under big cactus plants." But then he regretted his sarcasm. The doctor was only trying to help.

"Whatever it is, keep it up," said the doctor, ignoring Lorenzo's comments. "I'll drop by in the morning to see how you're doing. And I'll prescribe a pain med, in case you need it."

"Thanks, doctor. I appreciate your good care."

After the doctor left, Lorenzo used his cell phone to call Sam.

"No way!" said Sam when he heard what had happened.

"I'm fine—well, almost fine."

"Tell me what you need, boss, and I'll get it for you!"

"Thanks, Sam. I appreciate it. You do so much for me already that I hate to ask more of you."

"Boss, you got to be shittin' me," he said, a note of disgust in his voice. "With all you do for me every day? No way I can ever repay you!"

They agreed that Sam would look over the mail and review the phone messages, and then come to the hospital that night to bring him up-to-date. He could bring Jo and Tito along, but Lorenzo would only let Tito stay in the room for a few minutes.

"He's been asking lots of questions about you. Where you are, when you're coming home, that kind of thing."

"Poor little guy," said Lorenzo. "He's pretty confused, I'm sure."

"We'll be there about seven. Okay by you, boss?"

"Sure. Great. Don't tell Tito where you're going so he'll be real surprised when he sees me."

"Sure, boss. Good idea. See ya later. Call me if you think of anything else I need to do."

After he disconnected, Lorenzo's eyelids started getting droopy. He turned over in the bed and was soon in a deep sleep. About a half-hour later, a man wearing the white coat of a physician opened the door a crack and peered in. He was about to enter when a nurse came up behind him.

"Can I help you with something, doctor?"

"No, no. Nothing. I thought he was my patient."

As the man walked away, the nurse consulted a sheet of paper on her clipboard and shook her head. She walked quickly to the nurses' station and punched a few numbers into the phone on the console.

"Security," answered a gruff-sounding voice.

"Tim, we may have an intruder on Ward 5." She listened for a few seconds. "Yes, at the room assigned to the patient who was injured in the incident on the ferry. Okay, we'll see you soon."

She disconnected and walked back to Lorenzo's room. She opened the door and walked over to his bed. He was sound asleep and nothing seemed amiss.

🌿 🌿 🌿

Lorenzo woke up after an hour and got up to use the bathroom. He was walking back to the bed when an older nurse bustled in and almost knocked him over.

"Oh my goodness," she said, glancing at his naked rear end briefly exposed by his flapping nightshirt. "We mustn't get up on our own," she chirped.

"Tell me, Miss . . ." He glanced at her name tag. "Miss Pappas . . ."

"It's Ms.," she said, still looking at his exposed buttocks.

"Why don't these dreadful bed shirts have backs?"

"The better to see you in your natural state," said a younger nurse as she walked quickly into the room, pushing aside Ms. Pappas and happily ogling the rest of Lorenzo's private parts as he sat down on the bed and raised his legs to lie down.

"I've got this, Ivy," she said to the older nurse. "Why don't you take your break now?"

Ms. Pappas quickly left the room.

The younger nurse—Evelyn Baxter, according to her name tag— began straightening the sheet and blanket around Lorenzo's torso.

"There, that should be more comfortable for you," she purred. "Maybe you'd want to pull down your nightshirt too—under the covers, of course."

Women and men had been coming on to Lorenzo for years, but this was the first time by a nurse. They both started laughing. Just then, the door opened and Sam was standing there with a bouquet of flowers in one hand.

"Your son?" asked Ms. Baxter.

"Say what?" said Sam with a startled look on his face.

Both Lorenzo and Baxter laughed again.

"Sam's my legal assistant," explained Lorenzo, "and my good friend."

Sam walked hesitatingly into the room. "Did I break up something here?"

"No, no, just a little nurse/patient confab. Right, Mr. Madrid?" Baxter replied.

"That's it, a confab," said Lorenzo, agreeing with her. "See you later, Ms. Baxter."

Nurse Baxter walked out of the room, pausing to wink at Sam as she passed him.

"Wow and good gracious, as my grandma used to say," said Sam. "Who was that?"

"Just my devoted nurse."

"But you always told me that, you know, you swing the other way," said Sam.

"Oh, I do, Sam, when I swing at all," said Lorenzo with a smile. "But as my old boyfriend used to say, 'It doesn't cost anything to look'."

Sam walked over to the bed and handed Lorenzo a folder. "This is all . . ."

"Wait. Where is Tito?"

"He's outside with Jo," said Sam. "There's a play area for kids down the hall."

"Good idea. So, tell me what you've got."

Sam ran down the list of their two major and, so far, only cases. He had researched more material on adoption in Ecuador. He had the names of two couples who had been successful and the name of a single woman who had been unsuccessful.

"Good. I want to talk to them in my office next week—or we'll go to wherever they are. What's next?"

"The background work on Andy Corning's case is done. I researched every case I could find—or, I should say, that the law librarian at Willamette could find. I think you know more about that than I do."

"Yeah, of course I do," said Lorenzo. "I'll fill you in tomorrow, back at the office."

"You'll be well enough to come back tomorrow?"

"Yeah, I only got shaken up. But my car is gone—to the bottom of the Willamette River."

"No kidding?"

"No kidding. So, I want you to lease something for me fast."

"You got it, boss."

At that moment, the door opened and Tito came bounding into the room. "Papa, Papa," he shouted, as he leaped up onto the bed. Lorenzo groaned as the little boy landed full force on him.

"I am missing you so much," he shouted, as he kissed Lorenzo on both cheeks and snuggled next to him.

"A boy and his daddy," said Jo with a sigh.

Lorenzo sat up and pulled Tito around in front of him. "I think you have gotten bigger since yesterday when I last saw you," he said. "Have you been having fun with Jo and Sam?"

The boy leaned over to whisper into Lorenzo's ear. "They are good but not like you. You are my papa!"

As Tito said that, the thought crossed Lorenzo's mind that he might never be able to let go of this little boy. But he would probably have to.

Lorenzo pulled Tito close and kissed him on the forehead. "Okay, my little man, I'm going to let you and Jo and Sam go home. You need to eat so you can be strong for tomorrow when I come home and we play and play. Okay?"

Tito didn't look all that convinced, but he slid down off the bed and walked over to Jo. He looked up at her and said, "Let's go home."

"Leave that material with me, and I'll look it over before I go to sleep tonight," Lorenzo said to Sam. "I think I'll be released by nine or so. You'll have to pick me up since I don't have a car."

"That's right," said Sam. "I'll put getting you a car at the top of my list."

Later, after he ate a rather unappetizing dinner, Lorenzo looked at the material for a while, but it made him drowsy and he was soon asleep.

That was at about 10 p.m. He was sleeping so soundly at 2:30 a.m. that he didn't hear the short man dressed in the scrubs of an orderly open the door, silently cross the room, and pick up the folder that was lying on the bedside table.

CHAPTER

32

IT TOOK A WHILE BEFORE MAXINE REALIZED how bad the situation was that she had gotten herself into. The bravado she had displayed in her career—and her life—was useless in this situation. She was in a foreign country, attempting to get official documentation for something that had already been done. Tito had been taken from Ecuador to the U.S. illegally. Even if she had not actually taken him herself, she had sheltered him for over a year. In the eyes of the law, she had kidnapped him.

And now? The more she thought about her plight, the more upset she got. By the time the car arrived in Manta, a larger city on the Pacific Ocean, she was shaking with fear and frustration and hugging herself to ward off the cold. Try as she might, she could not hold off the tears. They ran down her cheeks.

When the car slowed down as they entered the city, she tried to calm down. Squaring her shoulders, she said softly, "I will survive this!" She dabbed her eyes and wiped her nose and repeated, "I will survive this!"

After driving a few more blocks, the car pulled up to a shabby-looking building with bars on the windows. One of the men opened the front door and walked to the rear.

A LORENZO MADRID MYSTERY

"I HAVE THE RIGHT TO CALL THE AMERICAN EMBASSY!" she yelled.

"*Señora,* you will remove yourself from the vehicle," said the guard. "Then you will follow me. *No perturbe.*"

Maxine got out and followed him into the building. The smell inside was overpowering. The combination of human sweat, urine, and cigar smoke made her gag.

"I HAVE THE RIGHT TO CALL THE AMERICAN EMBASSY!"

An older woman in uniform stepped up and grabbed her by the shoulder, propelling her through a door at the rear. Men and women, their wrists in shackles, lined the narrow corridor. Most were sitting with their legs stretched out in front of them, and she tripped and almost fell to the floor several times.

The uniformed woman pushed her into a small room, to the left where a male officer with a big mustache stood behind a desk. He motioned her forward and pointed to the large ink pad lying here. He held up both hands and wiggled his fingers.

She pressed her thumbs and fingers into the soft pad and made the impressions on his paper. With no towel to get rid of the ink stains, she wiped both hands on her skirt. He motioned her forward and handed her an old-fashioned slate board and a piece of chalk. "*Apellido.*" She carefully printed her last name in large letters on the black slate and handed it back to him.

Next, he pulled her in front of a dirty white sheet that was hanging on the wall. He stepped behind a camera mounted on a tripod and looked through the viewfinder. "*No sonrías.* No smiling." He motioned for her to stare straight into the camera and then to turn left and then right.

At that point, the woman reappeared and pulled Maxine out into the hall, to the left, and through a steel door with bars on a small window. Obviously, they were headed to the cells.

"I HAVE THE RIGHT TO CALL THE AMERICAN EMBASSY!" she shouted as the steel door clanged shut behind her.

118

CHAPTER

33

THE DUTY OFFICER AT THE AMERICAN EMBASSY in Quito had only been in the country for a week. A graduate of Georgetown University with a major in Spanish and Latin American government, he had been thrilled that his first assignment was in Ecuador.

When the phone rang at 2 a.m., he was so eager to carry out his new duties that he picked it up on the first ring.

"American embassy, Officer Boynton speaking."

The male caller spoke so fast that Boynton couldn't understand him.

When the man paused to breathe, Boynton replied, "Speak more slowly, *por favor. No comprendo. Ingles?*"

The man spoke again, this time in English and at a pace Boynton could understand. "There is this American lady. She has been arrested."

"Arrested? Where is she?"

"She is in a very bad jail in Manta. On the coast. Do you know Manta?"

Boynton was frantically looking at a map of the country on his computer to see where Manta was located. "Okay, I see it. Please stay on the line." Boynton punched a number into an intercom and waited.

A sleepy voice responded after one buzz. "Second secretary Kurt Jenkins. It's the middle of the night—is this important?"

"Oh, I think it is, sir. An American woman has been arrested in Manta, over on the coast," Boynton replied.

"How do you know this?"

"A Latino man on the phone."

"That would be Carlos Fuentes. Keep him on the phone—I'll be right there."

Jenkins was standing next to Boynton in five minutes. He grabbed the phone and spoke. *"Bueno. Cómo está, Carlos. Qué pasa?"*

It took a few minutes for Fuentes to tell his story. Jenkins listened and nodded and said "a huh" from time to time. At one point he covered the mouthpiece with his hand and whispered, "Carlos is a local guy we pay to keep us up-to-date on what's happening in Manta. Very dependable."

Then into the phone he said, "How long ago was this, Carlos?" He listened. "Less than one hour, you say? *Muy bien.* Stay where you are, and I'll get back to you."

He turned to Boynton. "An American woman has been picked up by the local police in Manta. Not sure what happened, but we've got to get someone up there as fast as possible."

"How will you do that?" Boynton asked.

Jenkins shrugged his shoulders and pulled out a card from his wallet. "I'll tell you that in a minute."

He glanced at the card and walked over to a cabinet and opened it.

"This'll be good for you to know," he said to Boynton. He held up a tiny earpiece and inserted it into his ear. A small microphone dangled down in front of his mouth. He punched some numbers into a unit on the shelf and said, "Quito Base calling Roving 6."

He turned back to Boynton. "We've got a few operatives in the field on various assignments. There's a team near Manta, and I'm calling the leader."

They both waited. Within seconds, the unit emitted a crackling sound.

"Yo, Curtis," Jenkins said. "Got a hot one. What is your location?"

Jenkins listened then spoke. "Okay, here's what you're going to do and do as fast as you can. You know the jail in Manta?" He listened. "Good. An American woman is in the jail there. I don't know why and, at this point, it doesn't matter. We'll clear it up later with the *federales* here. Just get her out of there and get her here to Quito. You got transport?" Pause. "Good deal. And Curtis? I don't even know her name. But she shouldn't be hard to find in that hellhole among all the prosties and pimps and drug dealers."

He listened for a moment or two then said, "Good luck, bro. I owe you big time on this one."

CHAPTER

"PAPA, PAPA," SHRIEKED TITO when Lorenzo walked into his house. "You have returned to me!" He ran over to Lorenzo and grabbed him around the legs.

Lorenzo leaned over and picked up the little boy, who began to kiss him.

"Easy, little man," said a slightly embarrassed Lorenzo. Part of him always held back displays of affection for fear of overstepping his limited role in Tito's life. Eventually, Maxine would return and take the boy home—that much was certain. But Lorenzo's growing love for Tito was equally certain.

He saw something of himself at that age—isolated and often afraid, vulnerable and in need of protection and love. Because he had not gotten much of either when he was growing up in East L.A., Lorenzo sought it in later life. He rebelled by being smarter than those he grew up with, including his parents, because he thought they would never understand him. And they certainly could not grasp his homosexuality.

"Good to have you home, Mr. Lorenzo," said Jo. "We've all missed you. How are you feeling?"

"Better now that I am home," he said, hugging Jo.

"What about me?" said Sam. "Am I some kind of disposable personage, destined to be treated like a piece of furniture?"

"What is a 'disposable personage'?" Lorenzo said, laughing. "You're sounding more and more like an attorney every day. I've created a monster!" They embraced. "But thanks for handling things here, my friend. You are definitely indispensable, not disposable."

"I leased you a Honda with lots of gadgets on it. Here are the keys and paperwork."

"Thanks, Sam."

"I've fixed some tea for all of us," said Jo, as she walked back into the room carrying a tray loaded with tea and cookies. "And milk for the little master here."

The four of them sat quietly for several minutes, drinking tea (and gulping milk) and eating cookies.

"Really good, Jo, thank you," said Lorenzo.

"Muy bien," said Tito, a milk mustache showing on his upper lip.

"Is that so?" said Lorenzo, who jumped up, grabbed the boy, and swung him around, the boy squealing with delight.

After he sat down, Lorenzo looked at Jo and Sam. "I've been overworking you. I know it and you know it."

They both shook their heads.

"No boss, we are here for you, always," said Sam. "Right, Jo?"

"Indeed we are, sir."

"You've given me the chance at a career I would only have dreamed about before we met," said Sam.

"I know that, and I appreciate all that you both do for me and for Tito," said Lorenzo. "Don't think I am saying goodbye or anything like that. I'm just giving you the weekend off."

The two of them exhaled quietly.

Lorenzo looked surprised. "Did you think I was letting you go? No way would I ever do that! Take three days and do something besides work."

"I'll go to Portland and visit the art museum," said Jo.

"I think I'll rustle up a date," said Sam. "What a concept that would be!"

"And what will you and the boy do?" asked Jo.

Lorenzo pulled Tito over to his side. "We're going to the coast. I think it's time to show Master Tito that his country does not have a corner on oceans. We have an ocean here in Oregon too. You need to see a lighthouse up close. You will love it."

As Jo and Sam were leaving, Lorenzo thought of something else. "Sam, do you have the folder containing all your research? I remember that you brought it to the hospital, but I've lost track of it."

"No boss, that's where I left it. You don't have it?"

"No. It must have gotten lost in the room somewhere. I'll call the hospital and see if it was turned in."

"Let me do that, boss. Happy to do that."

"If it doesn't turn up, can you remember the highlights?"

"Yes, sir, I can."

Sam and Jo left, and Lorenzo guided Tito into his office. "Sit down here. I want you to look at this book while I get ready for us to leave."

The boy sat in the small chair Lorenzo had bought for him and started turning the pages of the book, which was filled with photographs of every lighthouse in the state.

Lorenzo walked into the kitchen, punched in a number on his cell phone, and spoke. "Thaddeus Sampson, please." He listened then said, "Would you give me his voice mail?"

The recording device kicked in.

"Thad, it's Lorenzo. I need to talk to you about that client you referred me to. There've been several incidents. I might be in danger. Call me at your soonest chance. I'll be out of town, but I need to talk to you."

He disconnected the call and punched in another number.

"Drug Enforcement Agency. How may I direct your call?"

"Greg Nettles, please."

"Can I say who's calling?" asked the receptionist.

"Oh, we're friends," said Lorenzo. "I just wanted to see if he's free for lunch tomorrow."

"Of course," she said. "I'll put you through."

The DEA man picked up on the second ring. "Greg Nettles."

"Hi Greg. It's Lorenzo. How are you?"

"I'm good . . . or I was until I took your call," he said, laughing.

"I need to see you as soon as possible," said Lorenzo.

"Sounds serious."

"Yeah, maybe," said Lorenzo. "Do you still have that little cabin near Heceta Head?"

"Yeah. Want to come for a visit?"

"Yes. This weekend. Maybe tomorrow?"

"Okay. You have the address?"

"I do. I'll see you about noon, but I'll call first."

CHAPTER

THROUGH AN EXCHANGE OF MESSAGES, Lorenzo wound up asking Thad Sampson to dinner that night. Lorenzo felt that he owed Thad for recommending him to Andy Corning. But he also needed to tell Thad about the incident on the ferry, which he felt was connected to the case.

Lorenzo played soldiers with Tito for a while, and then got him interested in some picture books—one about the ocean and another one about whales. He lifted him up on a bar stool in the kitchen so he could cook and still talk to Tito.

"You know a lot of things," Tito said at one point.

"Comes with age," replied Lorenzo. "I am very old."

Tito shook his head. "My *abuela* was old. Wrinkles on her face. You don't have wrinkles on your face."

"Look closer, Tito. They are there."

The boy continued to look at the books.

Lorenzo didn't cook very much and normally preferred to eat out. He often joked to his friends that he only prepared food from just a few recipes. But since Tito had come to live with him, he had become more conscious of nutrition.

Jo often cooked for the three of them, and Sam was a frequent guest.

For tonight, though, he was making spaghetti with meat sauce, a salad, and garlic bread for Tito and Thad. He even had ice cream and cookies for dessert.

The doorbell rang at 6:45. Tito beat Lorenzo to the door and opened it. Thad Sampson seemed surprised when he saw the boy, but recovered quickly.

"Hello, little man," he said, kneeling down in front of the boy and shaking his hand.

"I'm not little," said Tito. "I'm big!"

Lorenzo got to the door and said, "Tito, this is Thaddeus Sampson, an old friend of mine. I wanted him to meet you since we are *compadres.*"

"You are black, and I am brown," said Tito to Thad. "I have never talked to a black man like you."

"Well, it's time that you did," said Lorenzo, reaching for the bottle of wine Thad had in his hand. "Come in."

He turned to the boy. "Please take Mr. Thad's coat and put it on my bed."

The boy took the coat and skipped away to do just that.

Thad followed Lorenzo into the living room. "Nice digs. Are you renting or buying?"

"Leasing for a year," said Lorenzo. "I'm never sure what I will be doing next."

"Or who you'll be doing it with," said Thad, shaking his head. "You know I could still be that guy."

"Not now, Thad. I'm still trying to figure out my career. And now, with the boy, my life has taken a real unexpected turn."

"Is she ever coming . . ."

At that moment, Tito ran into the room, another book in his hand.

"Mr. Thad, will you read to me?"

"He would love that," said Lorenzo, "and I'll get dinner on the table."

❦ ❦ ❦

The meal turned out well enough. Between bites, Tito regaled them with stories of Ecuador. Although he did not know his family, he seemed to know a lot of people in Montecristi. Lorenzo guessed that many in the small town had looked after him unofficially. He spoke of "aunt" so and so and "uncle" so and so, but they were probably not related to him. He was a true orphan.

At 8:45, Tito yawned and that was Lorenzo's signal to put him to bed.

"I'll just be a little while," he said to Thad.

"I'll clear the table," Thad replied.

Lorenzo helped Tito put on his pajamas and supervised the brushing of his teeth. When Tito leaped into bed, he motioned for Lorenzo to lean over.

"What a great kiss," said Lorenzo, smiling.

"I like Mr. Thad," Tito whispered. "Can he come and play with us again?"

"Yes, little man, I promise. Are you too tired for a story?"

Tito did not answer but rolled onto his side and was soon snoring softly.

۷ ۷ ۷

Later, Lorenzo and Thad ate their ice cream and drank their brandy in the living room.

"How'd you get this place into shape so fast?" asked Thad, looking around. "You've put nice touches all around the room."

"I've got a great assistant, Sam Lincoln, who can do anything, whether it's legal research or moving furniture. I met him last year during my Hollywood misadventure."

"So, what's on your mind?" asked Thad. "As much as I love spending time with you, I don't think you invited me here just to enjoy your spaghetti and your company."

"Yeah, you're right. It's about that case you got me into with Andy Corning."

"I figured," said Thad. "Not an easy thing to handle. Bring me up-to-date."

For the next half-hour, Lorenzo told Thad about his visits with Corning, his stepmother, and the judge.

"The stepmother's quite a piece of work. Her son was there too, but he didn't say anything at first. A rough-looking guy stepped forward at one point and restrained the son when he came at me. She introduced him as Nick Conte, her 'chief of staff.' He looked more like a body-guard. She basically told me to back off and I refused. We did not part on good terms."

"Renzo, Renzo, Renzo," exclaimed Thad. "I can't ever let you out on your own! Are you in any kind of jeopardy because of all of this? I mean, I was just trying to pass along a client because I knew you didn't have very many."

"Make that *any* clients," said Lorenzo, shaking his head. "And I so appreciate it."

"Tell me about your meeting with Judge Browning after I left."

"We talked about Andy's situation in general, and I asked her about his chances of getting released. She was noncommittal but sympathetic. Then, the stepmother and her son barged in unannounced...."

"Wow! I can't believe it!"

"Oh yeah, there she was, shouting and threatening both me and the judge."

"So much for keeping Andy locked up," Thad said, shaking his head. "He'll be on his way to freedom as soon as a hearing is held. Good job, Renzo."

"Yeah, I'm pretty happy about how things seem to be turning out," he said. "But I need to tell you about something else."

"From the look on your face, I gather that the 'something else' involved something bad."

"Yeah, I guess. A truck ran my car off the Buena Vista Ferry two days ago."

"A TRUCK DID WHAT?" shouted Thad.

"I decided to take the scenic route back to Corvallis and thought of how pleasant it would be to cross the river on a ferry. I drove the car on board and was enjoying the ride, when all of a sudden the driver of a huge truck, who had driven up behind me, gunned his engine and pushed my car off the ferry!"

"Good God! Were you hurt?"

"Only a small cut on my head. I spent that night in the hospital in Corvallis."

"Any idea who it was?"

"I've got a pretty good guess."

"Mrs. Corning's so-called chief of staff," Thad suggested.

"I'm pretty sure it was him or someone hired by him," said Lorenzo. "He must have followed me from the courthouse. I didn't see him there, but I'll bet he was waiting outside."

"Obviously, Mrs. Corning doesn't want Andy to be released from the clinic," said Thad. "That's pretty blatant. Will you tell the judge?"

"Not yet. Besides, I can't prove anything."

"There's got to be more to this than just keeping Andy from managing the company," continued Thad. "So, how'd you keep from drowning?"

"I held my breath, escaped the car, and got to the surface as fast as I could."

"Did you see the guy driving the truck?"

"He was long gone by the time I got my head above water. And everyone else was running toward me, so it was easy for him to slip away."

"What about the cops? Did anyone show up?"

"The county sheriff was there in a half-hour or so. Took my statement and was going to interview me at the hospital the next morning but didn't show up."

"I'll talk to a close friend with the state police to see if there was a report or if anyone else heard about it. This isn't something that happens very often." Thad looked at his watch and rose from the chair. "I've got to get going," he said. "Got an early meeting in the morning."

As Lorenzo walked him to the door, he remembered what else he wanted to tell Thad. "Oh yeah, there's one more thing. Sam brought me a folder with work material to read while I was in the hospital.

The folder also contained information about Andy Corning. When I fell asleep, it was on the nightstand. The next morning, it was gone."

"That's very strange," Thad said. "You need me to protect you," he whispered, then kissed Lorenzo on the top of his head.

CHAPTER

AFTER HER INITIAL PROCESSING AS A PRISONER, Maxine was placed in a cell with ten other women. When she got to an empty section of the wall, she stopped and slid down to sit on the filthy floor.

"You don't understand, I am an American citizen," she kept saying to the disinterested guards. As one of them turned to leave, he leaned down and moved his index finger across his throat. *"Silencio!* Shut the fuck up!"

When she looked up, some of the women had gathered in a semicircle around her.

"No use cryin' or yellin' honey," said a Black woman who seemed older than the rest of them. "Ain't nobody gonna hear you or give a shit about you. You be here a little while, then taken to a real prison. This here's a jail. Believe me, there's a big difference."

"You know it, big mama," several of the women said in unison. "That is the God's truth!"

Maxine squared her shoulders and stood up. "Are all of you Americans?"

"Yes, ma'am," said the first woman, who the others called Big Bertha. "You got yourself in a real pickle if you in here, but we all in this together. You not alone."

At that moment, a Spanish woman pushed the other aside and stood in front

of Maxine.

"You might think you better than us, *bebe*, but you ain't," she hissed. "We cut yo' face if you disrespect us."

Big Bertha stepped in. "Now why you pickin' on our new friend here, Esmerelda? She ever done anythin' bad to you?"

"No, I guess not," said the Spanish woman. "But she might!"

"Well, I'll see that she doesn't cause any problems," replied Bertha. The group moved to the other end of the room.

Bertha leaned closer to Maxine. "We got your back while you here," she said. The others nodded and shouted, "YOU GOT THAT RIGHT!"

Bertha motioned for the others to gather around so the guards wouldn't hear her talking with Maxine.

"You get along better if you keep to yourself and follow the rules. You got a lawyer?"

Maxine shook her head. "This all happened so fast that I didn't have time to do anything. I kept asking to call the American embassy, but they ignored me."

"This place is in the sticks," said Bertha. "Way off the radar of the American embassy. You important or somethin' like that?"

"Not really," said Maxine. "I'm a journalist. Mostly I take photographs. I've been up in Montecristi."

"The Panama hat place," said Bertha. "A journalist, eh? I'd keep that to myself, if I was you. They'll think you're going to investigate them and get them fired or killed, and they might turn on you. You never know in this place."

The two of them talked for hours. Bertha had had an interesting life. She had come to Ecuador as part of a dance troupe and met an Ecuadorian man who had opened a bar in Manta. She had two kids and lived a good enough life until they got cholera and died.

"After that, I kind of gave up and started drinkin' when my husband started living with a local woman. One night when I was very drunk, I broke into her house and threatened both of them with a knife. That was two months ago, and now here I sit. I don't have no money to hire a lawyer and they keep postponin' my trial, so I'm stuck."

"I am so sorry for your trouble," said Maxine. "I wish I could help you."

Just then, the lights were turned off. A guard yelled *"SILENCIO"* and everyone quit talking. Soon, Maxine heard snoring coming from the other women in the cell. The thin blanket they had given her was useless against the cold, but she was so tired, she fell sound asleep anyway.

At 3 a.m., two men in hoods crept into the cell and pulled her to her feet. They placed a gunnysack over her head and half carried, half dragged her out into the corridor.

The guards turned toward the wall and ignored what was going on. Maxine was hustled to a vehicle and shoved into the rear compartment. The men removed the hood, put a gag in her mouth and tied it on, and blindfolded her. The door slammed and the van sped away as quickly as she had been driven in, with no one the wiser throughout the sleeping town. It was 3:15 a.m. The whole operation had taken only fifteen minutes.

CHAPTER

37

LORENZO CAREFULLY FASTENED THE SEAT BELT around Tito in the back seat of his car early the next morning for their ride to the coast.

"Why I don't sit with you, Papa?" Tito said, on the verge of tears. "You don't love me anymore?"

"No, no, Tito," Lorenzo said, kissing him on the head. "Of course, I love you very much. It is a rule—*muy importante* rule. Little kids like you have to be safe when they are in the car. If we crash . . ." He slammed his hands together with a loud clap. "I want you to be safe."

Tito was still sniffling so Lorenzo handed him a handkerchief. "Blow your nose, like this," he said and demonstrated with a loud blow.

"Okay," Tito said and blew his nose.

"Okay, we've got to get going. Here's a book about the lighthouse we're going to see on our trip. Take a look, and then we'll talk about it." He handed Tito a guidebook to the Heceta Head Lighthouse, which the boy took and started examining.

They drove out of Corvallis and were soon on Highway 20, the road to Newport. Once there, they would drive south on Highway 101 for about thirty minutes to Yachats, the town with the funny-sounding name where they would spend the next two nights.

Tito was quiet for a while and then he

started asking questions, very intelligent questions for a boy his age. "Why do we need lighthouses? Is the light like a light bulb in your house? Who sees the light? Why are they looking for it? Who lives in the lighthouse? Any kids? Where do they get food to eat? Where do they go to school? In the lighthouse? Is the lighthouse old? How old?"

Lorenzo was well-prepared for the questions, and he yelled the answers to Tito in the back seat.

"The Heceta Lighthouse is named for a real man, Tito, a Spanish man. His name was Hector Heceta, who came by ship to the same place we are going to see tomorrow."

"Will this famous man be there to say hello?"

"No, Tito. He died many years ago. Like over three hundred years."

"A very long time," said Tito.

"But he stayed there for only a little while and then sailed on to find other places to explore."

"Explore? What does that mean?"

"To search for new things in places no one has ever been before."

"Did he bring the light?"

"No, that came later. Men like to catch fish in the ocean waters next to the lighthouse, but the water is always rough."

Tito clapped his hands together. "Like that—like a crash?"

"Yes, just like that. But the water is so rough that ships had to be warned of the danger."

"So they didn't crash on the rocks?"

"Exactly. If they hit the rocks they would be torn apart and the men on board would be killed."

"And the fish would be lost."

"Exactly, Tito."

"So the light would protect them?"

"Yes. Because it shines day and night, the light shows the men on the ships that the rocks are there and that they need to stay away from them. And you know what? That light has been burning every day and night since 1894."

"A long time ago."

"Yes, Tito. A long time ago. We'll see it tomorrow."

"I will be happy to see it, Papa. Thank you for bringing me to this magical place."

This is really a great kid, thought Lorenzo.

❧ ❧ ❧

Lorenzo had known Greg Nettles for many years, both as a colleague who collaborated with him on several cases and as a friend who offered him protection when he needed it. Greg had acquired his cabin as part of a divorce settlement. It was located on several acres on the west side of Highway 101 about a mile north of the lighthouse. Married life had never been part of Greg's long-term plans. His career came first, which was something his three wives had not understood very well. All of them were rich, however, so Greg had received good settlements from the women, which they each in turn had gladly paid to be rid of him.

Tito woke up when Lorenzo turned onto the steep driveway that led to Greg's cabin.

"Papa. Are we okay? What is this place?"

"Don't worry, little man. We are going to see a friend."

"You have many friends, Papa. Will this man be friends with me too?"

"Yes, I know he will. How can anyone turn down the chance to meet the great Tito?"

The boy giggled.

As the car pulled to a stop in front of the cabin door, Greg emerged with a pistol in his hand.

"Whoa, whoa, whoa!" said Lorenzo, getting out of the car and putting up his hands in mock terror. "Glad I let you know we were coming!"

The two men shook hands. When Lorenzo lifted Tito out of the back seat, Tito extended his hand before Greg could do the same.

"I love a kid with manners, don't you?" Greg said to Lorenzo. "Parents don't teach their kids much of anything these days."

"Very true," said Lorenzo. "Now, are you going to tell me about the gun?"

"Before I do, I have to ask you . . . what's with the beard? I'm surprised you would let anything mar your matinee idol face!"

"It's my new look," Lorenzo said, laughing. "Less buttoned down and scruffier. Now, about the gun?"

"Oh yeah, the gun," Greg said, shoving it into the pocket of his jacket. "You know the kind of bad guys I deal with every day of my life. I've put many of them in prison, and they don't like me very much. Very few people know about this place, and I want to keep it that way. The gun makes me feel better about being here alone. Of course, I have used guns in my work for years. But I don't usually bring them out at home."

"Okay, that makes sense," said Lorenzo.

"Come on in," Greg said, holding the screen door open for them. "Welcome to my humble abode."

"Wow," said Lorenzo. "I didn't realize that you worked as a home decorator on the side."

A large stone fireplace dominated the two-story living room. Doors to other rooms, two on a side, were open to reveal bedrooms and a large kitchen. The antique furniture looked expensive. Indian rugs hung over the railing of a loft.

"My last wife is a decorator," said Greg. "She did all of this before she moved back to Vermont. I try to keep it up. After years as a real slob, her influence changed my ways."

"Nice," said Lorenzo.

"Hungry? I've got lots of food." Greg saw Tito's eyes sparkle. "How about an ice cream bar?" asked Greg.

Tito looked at Lorenzo. "A bar of ice cream?"

"It's ice cream frozen on a wooden stick with chocolate covering."

"May I, Papa?"

"Yes, of course. You've been such a good boy that you deserve this ice cream on a stick."

Greg took two ice cream bars out of the freezer and handed them out, then took out another one for himself.

Tito spied some large books on a table and walked over to them.

He turned to Lorenzo for permission to pick one up. Greg saw this and smiled at the boy. "Go ahead, Tito. You can read any book I've got."

"Just watch your ice cream," said Lorenzo, handing him a napkin.

After the boy had walked to the other side of the room, Greg sidled up to Lorenzo and spoke in hushed tones. "You gonna adopt this little guy? He's really cute and seems very smart. He doesn't say much, though."

Lorenzo nodded. "He's been through a lot."

"But what about the mom?"

Lorenzo quietly brought Greg up-to-date on Maxine's efforts to adopt Tito legally.

"Whew!" Greg said. "That's gonna be real hard. Especially in the current political climate, our new beloved president would see him as a terrorist or a drug dealer right from the get-go!"

"She's my client, and I'll try to help her when I can," explained Lorenzo. "She's in Ecuador right now, to see if she can adopt him legally."

"You said that her boyfriend, this Bickford guy, took him out of the country, just like that?" He snapped is fingers.

"That's what he did."

Greg shook his head. "Not very smart. If anyone finds out, his career in the military is over."

"She told me he's already under investigation, so the ax may have fallen by now."

"Are the two of them a couple?"

"Not legally. They were once an item, maybe, but not now—at least, that's what she says."

"Are you and she an . . . item?"

"No," said Lorenzo, shaking his head vigorously. "You know that I swing the other way, when I swing at all. I'm just trying to help both of them."

"But in the meantime, you've fallen in love with the boy and like having him call you Papa. Right, Lorenzo?"

Lorenzo smiled ruefully and nodded. "Yeah, I guess I do."

Greg poured them both coffee and placed the cups on a table between them. "But you didn't come over here to talk about foreign adoption. Knowing you, something else is on your mind."

"You know me too well, Greg. You're right. I think someone may be trying to kill me."

CHAPTER

38

CURTIS DESTEFANO HAD BEEN IN STATE DEPARTMENT SECURITY for ten years. Although he had been assigned to embassies all over the world, he preferred Latin American countries. He liked the weather and the people, and he spoke serviceable Spanish. He had been in Ecuador for two years, long enough to afford to live in nice quarters in a safe compound. He even had two girlfriends.

He had been fast asleep with his favorite, Consuelo, when he got the call from Kurt Jenkins.

"That's not real far from me," he said, trying unsuccessfully to stifle a yawn. "Did Fuentes call it in?"

"Yeah, he did. He's very dependable. What do you need?"

"I've got it all in my kit bag here: GPS, weapons, food, communications gear, the whole nine yards. I'll get my guys and be on my way ASAP."

"Good," said Jenkins. "Keep me posted."

"Oh yeah, boss. One more thing."

"Okay. Shoot."

"How high priority is this woman and this mission?"

"No VIP priority, for sure, but I don't think we want any kind of incident right now, so do this as fast as you can. Relations with the Ecuadorian government are always a bit strained. Their president has made vague anti-American speeches on and off for years. Like many small countries, they need us but they don't want to admit they need us so they play hard-to-get sometimes. And they really go ballistic when we do unilateral stuff— like you're about to do. But we can't mess around when the life of even one American might be in jeopardy. Just go get her and bring her out safely. I'll deal with the political fallout, if there is any."

"Okay, boss," said DeStefano. "I got it covered."

DeStefano spent the next hour rounding up his team of four: Eddie Green and George Napier, expert marksmen, Benny Porten, a medic, and C.J. Belinski, a communications guy. They soon raced out of their compound and were on the road to Manta.

🌿 🌿 🌿

The first rays of sun were shining through the trees when Napier stopped the vehicle on a hill just above the jail. DeStefano signaled for one of them to stay with the truck. The other four exited the truck and moved slowly down the hill to the jail.

With a concussion grenade in one hand, he pushed gently on the door with the other. Surprisingly, it opened easily. The four men moved quickly into the room and fanned out along the walls. It was empty.

As DeStefano moved toward the door at the rear, they glimpsed someone in the hall. They tensed, fingers on the triggers of their weapons. Their leader held up his hand.

"Jesus, Fuentes!" he said. "We almost shot you!"

"Hello to you too, Curtis. *Cómo está usted?*"

Curtis grabbed him with a hug. "I'm good! How are you, *amigo?*"

"Good, good."

"So, what do we have here?"

"We have the jailers tied up in a back room, and the cells are full of prostitutes."

"I resent that designation," said a loud voice at the rear of the building.

DeStefano walked toward the sound.

A group of about ten women were in the cell, some lying on dirty cots, some sitting on the floor, and others, like the one with the loud voice, standing next to the bars.

"And who might you be?" asked DeStefano.

"Bertha Domingo at your service, and I do mean at your service," she said. "You're cute for a white guy."

"Are you the spokesperson for these ladies?" he asked with a smile.

"I am that, *señor*. And much, much more."

"Okay. I believe an American woman was put in here with you yesterday. What can you tell me about her?"

"I can talk more freely if you let me out of this filthy hellhole."

DeStefano turned to Fuentes. "You seen any keys in this place?"

Fuentes disappeared into another room and came back with a large ring of keys. He fumbled around and, after trying several, found the right one.

DeStefano pulled the door open slowly. As he figured they would, several of the women pushed toward the opening.

"Not yet, not yet!" he shouted as Fuentes repeated the same command in Spanish. He pulled Bertha through and then slammed the door. The women began to shout and hiss at him.

"Tranquilo!" Bertha shouted, and they quieted down immediately.

DeStefano led her into a smaller room at the other end of the hall with a table and two chairs. He pulled out a chair on one side of the table for her and sat down in the one opposite her.

"Okay, *Señora* Domingo, tell me what you know."

"My friends call me Big Bertha, for obvious reasons," she smiled. "I could really use a Coke or a Fanta."

DeStefano got up and walked out into the corridor, which contained a soft drinks machine.

"Got any Ecuadorian money?" he said to Fuentes. The man inserted some coins and two bottles dropped out. He opened them with his teeth and handed them to DeStefano, who carried them back into the smaller room and placed one in front of Bertha. She picked it up and emptied it in one prolonged gulp. She wiped her mouth with the back of one hand.

"Okay, Mr. Boss Man, what do you want to know?"

"What did the American woman say to you?"

"She was really nice and didn't treat me like some kind of criminal. She seemed to realize that I chose this life for a reason. She was very scared and said she didn't know why she was picked up and put in here. Not a nice place for anyone, but certainly not a lady like her."

"So what happened next?"

"We all went to sleep. I mean, as much as you can sleep in a hellhole like this place. I heard a noise in the middle of the night and saw some guys in black hoods come in fast and drag her out real fast. I guess she was real surprised because she didn't say a thing. And they didn't say anything either. They didn't seem to want to hurt her but just wanted to get her out of here."

DeStefano stood up. "I don't know what you're in here for, but I'm going to let you and the other ladies go because you helped me and I appreciate that. Just get the hell out of town and don't look back. Okay?"

"*Muchas gracias!*" Bertha smiled and gave DeStefano a long kiss on his mouth before letting out a loud whoop and running back to the cell. He heard her talking to the others through the door. He walked out into the corridor and nodded to Fuentes to open the cell.

The women grabbed their belongings and ran quickly out of the building. The sun was melting the morning mist as they disappeared, running in all directions.

"I hope none of them are murderers," he said to his team.

CHAPTER

OUTSIDE OF TOWN, the men who had taken Maxine switched vehicles again. She was yanked from the back seat of one vehicle and hustled to the other vehicle. She heard a door sliding open and then slammed shut after she was inside.

"I DEMAND TO BE TAKEN TO THE AMERICAN EMBASSY!" Her gag had become loose, and she was able to keep shouting until her voice was so hoarse her throat hurt. "I AM AN AMERICAN CITIZEN! YOU CAN'T DO THIS TO ME!"

Then she smelled the sweat of someone in the back with her.

"Please help me. I have a child. I am a mother. If you have a kid, you must know the pain I feel!"

As the vehicle lurched down the road, she heard the man move until he was right next to her. *"Tranquilo!"* He moved the gag back up, over her mouth, and tightened the strings that held it in place, then he moved away from her.

Maxine had been in difficult situations before. Journalists who work overseas often face danger. But this was the first time she had felt hopeless. In the past, she had always gotten out of whatever mess she was in. This time, though, no one knew where she was. No one would know what had happened to her. She could be killed

and buried, and have her decomposed body dug up by an animal years from now. By then, Tito would be a grown man and would have forgotten her—and so would everyone else. She could not let that happen. She decided to remain as calm as she could and wait for the next part of this terrifying journey to play out.

She dozed for a while and woke up when the vehicle stopped. She heard gates opening and then closing behind the vehicle as it entered some kind of structure. She heard men shouting and a woman scream.

The door opened, and the man in the vehicle with her pulled off the blindfold and removed the gag. She gulped down the water in the canteen he threw at her.

"More, *por favor.*"

He handed her another canteen of water, an apple, and a package of biscuits, which she ate quickly.

"Where am I? Who are you?"

He shrugged and got out of the vehicle. He looked like an indigenous Indian, with dark skin and black hair.

A man with the lighter skin and finer features of someone of Spanish descent walked up. He was dressed in a stylish suit and wore a tie and expensive-looking shoes.

"*Señora* March, I am Francisco Manteca, at your service." He bowed and clicked his heels together.

"Thank God. Someone who speaks English," Maxine exclaimed.

"I am always amazed when people like you come to another country and do not try to learn to speak the language of that country."

"You are right," she said. "I should have done that."

"Indeed, madam, you should have, especially when you embarked on such a complicated mission," he said, shaking his head. "It is no small feat to come into a country and try to justify the kidnapping of one of our citizens—a young boy, who I believe is called Tito."

Maxine felt faint but tried to hide her fear. "I have no idea what you are talking about. What do you mean? I am a journalist on assignment."

Manteca smiled and shook his head. "So many lies. Do all Americans lie like you, *Señora* March? Did you think we would not know it when you came to Quito to inquire about adopting the boy?"

"I . . . didn't . . . think . . ."

"You are right," he sneered. "You did not think. And how stupid did you think we were, not to know that this precious little boy was already in your country? Kidnapped! Taken away to God-knows-what kind of life!"

"We took him to a better life!" she said. "He was living in the streets of Montecristi, an orphan, forgotten by society and doomed to live in poverty. With me, he has a good home and clean clothes and the chance to go to good schools. Later, he will go to college and be able to achieve more than he ever could here in this . . . this . . . third world country."

As Maxine uttered those words, she knew immediately that she had gone too far. One does not insult a whole country to someone who is part of its upper class.

"I'm sorry," she said. "I get carried away sometimes."

"Indeed you do, *Señora* March," said Manteca. "And you are about to be carried away to a place where we put enemies of our country. Until your trial, you will be held in our most secure prison. Have you heard of Guayaquil?"

"No, I have not," she said, trying to keep from crying.

"It is on the coast, about 270 kilometers southwest of here," he said. "We have a prison there, where you will be joining our female drug offenders and all of our international prisoners. When you get there, you won't have to learn to speak Spanish because about a dozen of your fellow Americans will be there with you."

"I DEMAND YOU LET ME CALL THE AMERICAN EMBASSY!" she shouted. "THAT IS MY RIGHT!"

"I am afraid that there are very few rights where you are going," said Manteca. *"Adios."*

The goonish man returned and shoved her back into the vehicle. He threw more water and food to her and the door slammed again. Then the vehicle sped away with such force that she banged her head on the floor.

CHAPTER

40

SOMETHING WOKE LORENZO UP the following morning. When he opened his eyes, he saw Tito standing by the bed with a feather in his hand. Lorenzo sat up and made a growling sound and reached for the boy, who giggled and ran out of reach.

"Papa, Papa!" he squealed. "Do it again! Be a monster!"

There was more growling and lunging by Lorenzo, who sat up and grabbed the boy and held him.

"I love you, little man," he said.

"I love you also, Papa."

Lorenzo stood up and put on a T-shirt, pants, and a sweatshirt. "You need to put on some clothes too, my little pal."

He helped the boy take off his pajamas and put on jeans, a T-shirt, and his own sweatshirt.

"Okay, Tito. Let's see if that lazy bones Greg is up yet!"

"What means 'lazy bones'?" Tito asked.

"That is someone who wants to sleep all the time and not raise his bones—his body—out of bed. Like you are when I make you get up to meet Miss Jo."

"Yes, I see," Tito said, although Lorenzo was not sure he understood.

"Remember what I have told you about

'slang,' the funny things we say in English because we get tired of talking in such a grown-up way?"

"Yes, Papa. Maybe I get to this later in my English."

Lorenzo laughed and followed the boy out the door. Tito's hard life has taught him to adjust to whatever happens, he thought to himself. Quite a kid!

Greg was sitting at the kitchen table, looking at his I-phone, a cup of coffee in front of him. "Good morning, guys," he said. "Are you hungry?"

He rubbed his stomach and Tito nodded and rubbed his own stomach.

"*Si, Señor* Greg."

"Pancakes. Do you know pancakes?"

"We eat them a lot," said Lorenzo, pouring himself a cup of coffee and Tito a glass of milk.

They both sat down at the table and watched Greg prepare breakfast.

"I did a lot of the cooking when I was married," Greg explained. "My wife's idea of a good meal was to microwave a chicken pot pie or some lasagna. Yuck!"

The food was ready quickly. Greg piled pancakes on Tito's plate while Lorenzo added butter and syrup. Then he did the same for Lorenzo and himself.

Because the men had been so tired the night before, they hadn't talked about Lorenzo's troubles. And now, rather than talk in front of Tito, they talked about things that might interest him.

"You know what a lighthouse does?" asked Greg.

"Shows ships where the rocks are," Tito answered. "So they don't crash."

"Good. How about why a lighthouse is so tall?"

"So these ships can see the light. If it was on the ground, no one would see it, and then the ships would crash. Right, Papa?"

"Right, Tito."

They finished eating, and Lorenzo cleared the table of the dishes and stacked them in the sink.

"Okay guys," said Greg. "Let's walk down to the lighthouse. Are you ready, Tito?"

The boy nodded vigorously as Lorenzo put the boy's jacket and extra pants and T-shirt in his backpack.

They walked down Greg's road and crossed the highway at the entrance to Heceta Head, the state park that took its name from the lighthouse.

"We can talk while we walk and while the boy is preoccupied," said Greg.

Lorenzo nodded as Tito ran ahead, down the road to the parking area below the lighthouse.

"Be careful, Tito!" he shouted. "Don't get out of my sight. Be sure you can always see me. Okay?"

The boy ran ahead a bit farther but kept turning to look at the men. Both waved at him.

"So, what's this about someone trying to kill you?" asked Greg, shaking his head. "That's nothing new, is it? One person or the other has been trying to kill you since I first met you."

At that moment, Tito raced up the path. "Papa, Papa. Let's go!"

"I'll fill you in when we get to the lighthouse," Lorenzo whispered to Greg. "Okay, little man, let's go."

Saying that, Lorenzo ran down the path to meet Tito, picked him up in his arms, and whirled him around. The boy giggled until Lorenzo put him back on the ground.

"I'll race you," Lorenzo shouted and then sped down the path, the boy following and laughing. Greg brought up the rear.

At the bottom, Lorenzo led Tito to the tide pools that formed in the rocks along the shore when the tide was out. "Come over here," he said to Tito. "Look at all the little sea creatures that the ocean brings in."

"What is 'sea creatures'?" The boy peered into the pools.

"All kinds of things, like sea stars, hermit crabs, starfish, mussels, and all kinds of seaweed."

The more Tito looked into the pools, the bigger his eyes got. He

150

reached into one indentation and stirred up the water with one finger.

"Be careful not to disturb those little guys in there," said Lorenzo, kneeling down and putting one arm on Tito's shoulder. "This is their home—the place where they live."

He glanced over at Greg, who was smiling and shaking his head.

"Who knew that you had fatherly instincts."

Lorenzo stood up and laughed. "Or motherly ones." Then he turned back to the boy. "Tito, let's walk up to the lighthouse so you can see it, and then we can come down here later. Okay with you?"

"Yes, Papa. Okay with me. But we will come back here to this place? I love this place."

The three of them walked up the hill to the lighthouse, with Tito running ahead but always turning around to make sure the two men were following him.

At the end of the path, the ground was flat. The lighthouse and the keeper's house had been built here. They walked past the keeper's house, which was closed for the season, and on toward the lighthouse. It had been constructed at the edge of what, from a distance, looked like a shelf.

Lorenzo pulled out the guidebook he had brought along and began to read to Tito and Greg, who both sat down on a bench.

Lorenzo looked around. "Glad no one else is around today. I don't need an audience," he said. "Okay, here's what it says. The lighthouse was opened in 1894, as I told you. It is maybe the shortest lighthouse on the Oregon coast—like you, Tito. At over 56 feet tall, it is not as tall as some of the other lighthouses on the Oregon coast, but because it is high on a cliff, the ship captains can see the light as far as 21 miles out to sea."

He turned to the boy. "And why is that, little man?"

"So ships will not crash into the rocks." Tito turned and pointed down the steep cliff. "Down there."

"Good boy," said Lorenzo.

"The construction started in 1892, and 56 men worked here," he continued. "Because this place is hard to get to, the lumber came in by boat. The stones had to be brought here by wagon."

He looked at Tito. "You know what wagon means?"

The boy shook his head.

"It's what people used to haul things around. They were pulled by horses."

The boy nodded his understanding.

"The light could not be turned on with a switch. The man in charge—called a keeper—lighted kerosene, and the flame was reflected through a very big lens." Lorenzo turned toward the structure. "See it up there?"

Tito stood up and walked toward the building. "Yes, Papa, I see."

"Okay, that's enough of this, guys. Let's go inside and walk up to the top."

The three of them went in and took the guided tour of the light-house. The views were spectacular, and Tito seemed in awe of every-thing. It occurred to Lorenzo that in the boy's hard life, there had been no time for anything but survival.

Then they walked back down the hill and stopped at the tide pools.

"Go ahead, Tito. You can play in the water. We'll be right here. Just be careful of the slick rocks."

Lorenzo and Greg sat down at a nearby picnic table.

"Okay, Lorenzo," said Greg. "Are you going to tell me what the hell you were talking about earlier?"

"It all started with a new client, Andy Corning. His stepmother had him committed to a mental clinic so she could take over the business he thought he would inherit. He has hired me to get him out, and that's what I'm working on. The stepmother, of course, doesn't want that to happen. And now, I can't prove it but I think she's hired someone to stop me, maybe even kill me."

Then Lorenzo told him about the incident on the ferry and the folder being taken from his hospital room.

"Did you report these?"

"Oh yeah. The sheriff came to the ferry, but I was too shook up to give him an interview. He was supposed to come see me before I was discharged from the hospital, but I never saw him. So nothing was done, as far as I can determine," said Lorenzo.

"Do you think it was someone hired by this evil stepmother?"

"She introduced a guy at our meeting as her chief of staff," he said. "His name is Nick Conte. Maybe he's involved somehow."

"I'll check him out," said Greg.

"Hard to believe, but I can't think of anyone else who hates me enough to try to kill me," said Lorenzo, shaking his head.

"Except the drug guys you helped put in prison."

"But Esteban Perez is in witness protection," said Lorenzo. "You and I helped him get there. You think someone else in his . . ."

"That's exactly what I think," said Greg. "You'll need to watch your back and watch out for the boy!"

CHAPTER

AFTER SPENDING THAT NIGHT WITH GREG, Lorenzo and Tito headed back to Corvallis early the next afternoon. Greg agreed to check with his police sources to find out more about Nick Conte and his relationship with Andy Corning's stepmother. He also promised to inquire about how Esteban Perez was doing in the Witness Protection Program. "I can't find out where he is, of course, nor do I want to know," he had said, "but I can find out if he has caused any trouble. You know, some of these guys can't stand the isolation, so they come out of hiding and are soon back in trouble."

After Lorenzo buckled Tito into the back seat, they waved goodbye to Greg and pulled onto Highway 101. The drive to Waldport took fifteen minutes and he turned right at the only signal in town.

Because it was a sunny day, Lorenzo decided to take the long way back to town. Highway 34 ran from the small city of Waldport to Philomath, the town nearest Corvallis. It was slow going because the road was narrow and had a lot of curves, so tourists travelling to the coast usually took Highway 20, a more direct route that had recently been improved.

Traffic was light, with no other vehicles in sight but logging trucks, which were headed in the other direction. From the back seat, Tito sang what Lorenzo supposed was an Ecuadorian song until he fell asleep.

Lorenzo thought of the pleasure he had felt in taking care of Tito these past weeks and teaching him about the world. Jo was training him in language, writing, math, and many other subjects, but Lorenzo was teaching him about life. Although he knew he would have to give up Tito when Maxine returned, he hoped to be able to continue to see him often.

Lorenzo had never wanted to be with anyone—male or female—permanently enough to adopt a child. But having Tito around made him realize for the first time what he had missed.

After they had passed the small town of Alsea, Lorenzo noticed a big pickup truck behind him, perhaps a quarter of a mile back. He kept to his moderate speed, figuring that the driver would pass him at the next passing lane.

Several miles later, the driver seemed to accelerate so Lorenzo slowed down to allow him to pass. He was certainly in no hurry to return to town and all the pressures of his life.

Soon, however, the truck was right behind him and accelerating fast. A minute later and the driver was touching the rear bumper and then backing off, as if to push him off the road.

"Not again! First the ferry, now here," muttered Lorenzo. "What the hell!"

He stepped on the gas and moved ahead quickly, but the truck caught right up to him and began to ram him hard. It was all Lorenzo could do to keep the car on the road.

The noises woke up Tito, and he began to cry. "Papa, Papa!" he wailed. *"Qué pasa!"*

As they approached a side road, Lorenzo spotted an Oregon State Police cruiser sitting there watching for speeders. He turned abruptly into that road and barely avoided hitting the cruiser.

The truck roared past and was soon out of sight.

The trooper got out of his car and walked up to Lorenzo's car as he rolled down his window.

"License and insurance card please, sir," the trooper said. "Do you mind telling me what you thought you were doing?"

"Didn't you see that truck behind me? He was trying to run me off the road!"

"I only saw you turning in here, where I was parked," the trooper said. "I thought you were going to hit me. I have to say, sir, that you were driving like a crazy person."

"Yeah, I guess I was, but when you're being chased by a crazy guy in a huge truck, you react without thinking. I saw you and all I could think of was to get to you, so I made a try for it."

As the trooper walked back to his car to run a check on Lorenzo's record, Lorenzo yelled back to him. "Can I get my little boy out of the back seat?"

The trooper waved his assent. Lorenzo got out, opened the rear door, unhooked Tito, and lifted him up and out. He was still sobbing.

"That's okay, little man," said Lorenzo, holding him close. "I've got you." He reached over and dabbed at Tito's eyes. "Let me give you some water and a snack." They walked around to the front and Lorenzo put the boy on the passenger side, then gave him some water and a peanut butter cracker.

"Mr. Madrid," said the trooper, walking up to Lorenzo, "you checked out, and you're free to go. Sorry for the inconvenience."

"No apology needed . . ." Lorenzo glanced at his name tag, "Trooper Kaplan. You saved me from God-knows-what. That guy was trying to run me off the road, no doubt."

"I'm sorry, sir, but with no license number, there's no way to check him out."

"I'm not sure he even had a plate on that truck."

"I'll put this incident in my daily report and maybe the guy will try this again."

"Fair enough. Thanks."

The two shook hands, and Lorenzo buckled Tito into the back seat. When he pulled back onto the highway, he was relieved to find other cars on the road in both directions.

Lorenzo had decided that telling the trooper about the earlier incident with another truck was pointless. It would only complicate things.

As soon as he got home, he would call Greg and Thad. They needed to know that someone was doubling down on getting him off the Corning case . . . or killing him.

CHAPTER

MAXINE WAS SHIVERING by the time they reached their destination, both because of the night temperature and her fearfulness. The vehicle stopped in a courtyard. Buildings of five or six stories surrounded the open space. She could hear voices from above, in both Spanish and English, resonating from the forbidding walls. Women were shouting through barred windows from which laundry hung, fluttering in the breeze.

"Out, out, out," shouted a man in uniform.

Maxine stumbled out of the vehicle and almost fell in the mud until she steadied herself and found her footing.

"Ven aqui! Rapido! Rapido!" He led her to a door and pushed her through it. The small room was empty except for a young female guard sitting at a battered desk. The woman pointed to a chair and Maxine sat down.

"No *Español*," she said, biting her lip to keep from crying.

"I speak English, *Señora* Marsh."

Maxine let the mistake go. What did it matter?

"You have been arrested for kidnap- ping an Ecuadorian boy and will be held here until your trial," the guard said, read- ing from a paper she had in front of her.

"You have the right to hire an attorney, but the attorney must be a citizen of Ecuador."

"I want to call the American embassy," Maxine said. "I have a right to call my embassy!"

"In due course, madam," said the woman. "In due course."

"How do I get an attorney, and when and where can we meet?"

"This will all be explained to you in due course," the woman continued. "Now we must get you settled into a cell."

She pressed a buzzer, and a door behind her opened and an older woman walked into the room. This woman had what Maxine had always thought of as "mean" eyes, unblinking and unsympathetic.

"What do we have here?" the second woman said. "Another snooty American who thinks she can ignore our laws and kidnap our children?"

"I didn't kidnap Tito," Maxine said, exasperation in her voice. "He is better . . ."

"Save it for the court," said the woman. "Follow me."

Maxine stood up and did as she was told.

Behind the door, a long hall stretched as far as she could see. Halfway down, they stopped at another door marked Laundry and went in. All of the women in the room stopped working and stared at her.

A blond woman walked over and held out her hand to Maxine. "Dawn Young. I won't ask how you are because I'm sure you're feeling worse than on any other day of your life," she said, patting Maxine on her arm.

Dawn turned to the guard who had brought Maxine in. "I'll take it from here, Rosario. *Gracias.*"

The guard left.

"Have some water, er . . ."

"Maxine. Maxine March."

"Let's sit down." Dawn pointed to a desk and chairs in the back of the room, set away from the washers and dryers.

After they were seated, Dawn placed a single sheet of paper on the desk in front of Maxine. "Fill this out for me. It's not official, but I insisted that we keep our own record of who is in here. Just put down your name and your town but not the exact home address. You never know who might read this and who they might send to extort money or something worse. Put next of kin and/or who to contact. Again, no specifics."

Maxine wrote down her basic information and handed the sheet to Dawn.

"Good. They are supposed to send this to the embassy, but they don't always do that."

"Don't I get a call to the embassy?"

"In your dreams, honey lamb," said a large woman whose arms were covered with tattoos.

"This is Sandra," said Dawn with a smile. "She's not as tough as she looks."

"I am really a concert pianist and a gifted poet," Sandra scoffed. "I look the way I do to keep the predators away."

Maxine and Sandra shook hands.

"The guards are pretty lazy, so we run this section of the prison," said Dawn. "They only come alive if someone gets out of line. And the young ones hang around our young girls for sex from time to time."

"You're not that old, but you look mature so they won't bother you," Sandra said, laughing. "We're too old and hard-looking for that."

"Speak for yourself, Sandra," said Dawn.

"And they are afraid of us because we're lesbians . . . or at least we pretend to be," continued Sandra. "Scares the hell out of the Ecuadorians."

"Okay, enough of this small talk," said Dawn. "Let's get you settled in. And get you some clothes. They don't issue orange prison garb here, like in the U.S. You wear what you got. Jeans and sweatshirts are best. It's pretty cold in here most of the time. Tennis shoes or boots and lots of socks. You'll need to go with a layered look. Sandra will fix you up."

Maxine stood up and shook Dawn's hand.

"See you around," Dawn said. "Keep your wits about you, and you'll survive. You're lucky to be in our section of this awful place. We're all considered 'international'—in for drug possession mostly. The other sections are hell on earth. From what I've seen and heard, the conditions there are really bad."

"Urgent call for you from the States, boss."

Curtis DeStefano had been asleep with Consuelo for several hours and didn't appreciate the early morning wakeup.

"What the fuck!" he said to Boskin, one of the enlisted men who worked for him.

"A call. He's on the radiophone."

DeStefano groaned and patted Consuelo on her rear end. "Be back soon, darlin'." He got up and walked into the large room that was next to his sleeping quarters. "What's up? Do you know who it is?"

"No, boss, but the guy is pretty persistent. Says he needs to speak with you right away."

DeStefano picked up a headset and spoke into the microphone. "This is Curtis."

"It's about time," said a loud voice on the line. "This is Colonel Paul Bickford. I'm in Special Ops."

"Yes, colonel. What can I do for you?"

"I understand you botched the rescue of someone I love very much, Maxine March."

"I wouldn't say that we botched it, colonel. We just missed her. The bad guys got her out of the jail that we broke into and . . ."

"Sounds like a fucked-up operation to me! What are you going to do to set it right?"

161

CHAPTER

SINCE RETURNING FROM THE COAST A WEEK AGO, Lorenzo had busied himself with preparing for the competency hearing that he hoped would get Andy Corning released from the psychiatric clinic. With no more incidents involving the man in the pickup truck, he relaxed a bit and returned to his normal routine. Greg Nettles was making discrete inquiries about the driver but had, so far, not turned up anything.

With the office finally in order, Sam spent his time doing research for Lorenzo and studying for his entrance exams for law school. He hoped to attend Willamette or Lewis & Clark, but he knew that his GPA from college might be too low to qualify. Lorenzo vowed to pull any strings he could when the time came, and letters of recommendation from Lorenzo's friends Thad Sampson and Victoria Soto of the immigration law center in L.A. would help.

Tito's classes with Jo were going very well. Even though he had not attended any kind of school in Ecuador, Tito was very smart. His mind was like a sponge, retaining everything he read and heard. He had picked up English easily, both speaking and writing it. He was also good at math and was very interested in science and history. He was full of questions about the ocean and tide pools and lighthouses. Jo had to ask Sam to get more books from

the library and made it a point to download material for Tito from the Internet.

Lorenzo knew that the time was fast approaching when he would have to enroll Tito in a regular school, probably a private one where he would get the special attention not always possible in public schools, but for now, Jo was doing a wonderful job of teaching the eager boy.

The competency hearing was scheduled for 10 a.m. in Judge Browning's courtroom. Her clerk had made it clear that the change in locale had only do with logistics, not any change of status for the case.

Lorenzo met Andy Corning in the hall outside the judge's courtroom in the Marion County Courthouse. Andy looked rested and relaxed and was dressed in an expensive-looking suit, white shirt, and navy-blue tie. He had even managed to get a haircut. Sally Rizollo, the head nurse at the clinic, was with him.

They shook hands all around.

"I'm surprised to see you here, Nurse Rizollo," Lorenzo said.

"I'm the one who has supervised his rehabilitation," she said, her eyes flashing as if he was questioning her status.

Lorenzo put up his hands. "No need to be defensive. I just thought you'd be too busy to get away from the clinic."

"Mr. Corning is important to me," she said. "I want to make sure his condition is explained thoroughly and his recovery carefully discussed."

"You're talking as if I wasn't here!" said Corning. "Don't I get to be a part of the discussion? It's me who's suffered!"

Lorenzo motioned for them to sit down on a bench, then spoke to Andy. "It's your confinement that's the point here. I'd be happy if you did not have to talk at all. I want to let them show what they've got—which is nothing, really—and then I'll figure out how to respond. If you do testify, Mrs. Corning's attorney will try to provoke you into an outburst. Don't walk into that trap. Just smile and answer truthfully but with as few details as possible. Don't volunteer anything."

He told them what to expect and told Corning not to worry. "The facts are on your side," he said.

At that moment, the clerk opened the door and motioned for them to enter. As they did, she lingered, looking up and down the hall.

"Where is Mrs. Corning?" she said to Lorenzo.

"I have no idea."

They walked down the aisle, and the clerk directed them to one of the two tables inside the bar.

"Sit here. I'll be right back," she said, walking through a side door that presumably led to the judge's chambers. Within seconds, the judge walked in and stepped up to the bench.

"It would appear that not all parties are present," she said, a disgusted look her face.

Just then, the door to the courtroom burst open and Annabella Oglethorpe Corning stepped into the room, followed by her son Peter. She was dressed as if attending a fashion show or high tea. Her silk dress clung to her in all the right places, as the old clichéd phrase goes, and was set off by four strands of pearls and a lace shawl. Her hair had been carefully done up, with diamond-studded pins protruding from it.

"Nice of you to join us, Mrs. Corning," said the judge icily. "Please be seated." The judge looked back at the door. "Will your attorney be late too?"

"I fired him earlier today," Mrs. Corning replied. "I will be acting as my own attorney. I read for the law in my native Great Britain, so I feel perfectly competent to handle this . . . this . . . hearing or whatever you call it."

Lorenzo could sense that the judge was becoming even more irritated with Mrs. Corning.

"I urge you not to continue to show contempt for this court," said Judge Browning. "You need to respect the law, even when you don't agree with its findings."

"It sounds to me like you've already made up your mind in this case," said Mrs. Corning.

The judge banged her gavel. "No, I have not, but you are pushing me to a decision faster than I anticipated. Now sit down and listen to these proceedings!"

Mrs. Corning opened her mouth to speak, but the judge cut her off. "Bailiff!" One of the bullet-headed sheriff's deputies moved behind Mrs. Corning, who quickly sat down.

"Competency hearing for Andrew James Corning is now convened in the Third Circuit Court of Oregon, Judge Constance Browning presiding," said the clerk.

"Mr. Madrid, you may begin," said the judge.

After handing the judge and Annabella Corning a copy of his remarks, Lorenzo presented the facts of the case. "I would be happy to answer any questions you might have," he said in closing.

The judge shook her head. "No questions. This seems a thorough narrative."

"I have a question," said Mrs. Corning. "Why isn't your client wearing a straitjacket? Everyone seems to forget that he tried to kill me."

"Evaluations by two psychiatrists found that Mr. Corning is free of any anger issues he displayed before," said Lorenzo.

"ANGER ISSUES!" screamed Mrs. Corning. "It was much more than that! He tried to . . ."

"Yes," interrupted the judge, "so you have told us on numerous occasions. I think there is sufficient security in this room and in this building to prevent that from happening. Now, are you expecting any experts to speak on the matter at hand, which is your stepson's readiness for release?"

Mrs. Corning stood up. "I will be acting as my own expert witness. And my son Peter will assist me. He was there when Mr. Andrew Corning attacked me. Stand up, Peter!"

Peter stood up, looking embarrassed.

"I object, your honor," said Lorenzo, standing up. "That has not been proven. And I have to ask Mrs. Corning why she did not press charges at the time and have my client arrested. Instead, she had him committed to a mental institution under false pretenses so she could take control of a business his father had intended him to run!"

Annabella Corning exploded with rage and rushed over to Lorenzo and slapped him hard across the face. She seemed poised to do more but stopped.

"MRS. CORNING!" shouted the judge. "My patience is at an end. Bailiff, remove Mrs. Corning from my courtroom and take her to the holding cell!"

The bailiff led a sobbing Annabella Corning from the courtroom, followed by a confused-looking Peter.

"I have to say that I have never had anyone disrupt my courtroom in that manner in all my years of wearing these robes. Now that we have order, you may proceed, Mr. Madrid."

Lorenzo ended by summarizing the psychiatrists' reports, Nurse Rizollo's observations, and a report of the psychologist who met with Andy several times a week during his time at the clinic.

"I have nothing else, your honor."

"Given your thorough reporting and Mrs. Corning's lack of evidence, her disdain for my court and, I might add, her histrionics, I am ready to rule. Please stand, Mr. Corning."

Andy and Lorenzo stood up.

"Mr. Andrew Corning, I hereby release you from your involuntary confinement at the Cascade Clinic, effective immediately. You are free to go. Good luck."

Corning hugged Lorenzo and even Nurse Rizollo, and the three of them walked out into the hall.

"I'll have your things sent to the address we have on file," Nurse Rizollo said. "Good luck to you, Andy."

"It has been less of a nightmare for me because of your help," he said, hugging her again. "Thanks."

"Where can I take you?" Lorenzo asked Andy.

"I'm going to call my wife to pick me up," he said. "You can drop me at the entrance to the Willamette campus. I'll walk to the library and meet her there. We're going to be staying in a hotel in town tonight, to get reacquainted."

On the short ride to the campus, Corning thanked Lorenzo repeatedly.

"Just doing my job, Andy. Did you know you're the first client at my new law firm?"

"No, I didn't," he said. "I'm sure you'll be getting a lot more business in the future. I've got lots of Yuppie friends who always need a good attorney."

"Sounds good to me," said Lorenzo. "Keep in touch."

As Lorenzo headed out into the Salem rush hour traffic, he did not notice the vehicle that was following him several cars back. This time it was not an over-sized pickup but a black SUV.

CHAPTER

MAXINE HAD SETTLED INTO A DAILY ROUTINE, if any day could be considered routine in the living hell of a South American prison. Being in the section for international women helped a bit. The food was tolerable, the guards were less inclined toward physical abuse, and her fellow inmates—mostly being held on drug charges—were intelligent and attractive. The women did not know the extent of anyone else's charges or sentences, if any. It was an unspoken code between inmates that no one ever asked.

Maxine worked in the laundry with Dawn Young, the woman who had befriended her on the first day, and the fearsome but gentle Sandra, whose last name no one knew. The three shared a cell, which was Spartan but clean, and worked side-by-side washing endless loads of dirty sheets and towels in ancient washing machines that broke down at least twice a week.

When that happened, an old man whose face looked like it had been carved out of stone would arrive to go through the motions of fixing the washer, although his finishing touch was always a kick to the offending machine. The other women in the laundry kidded Sandra that Felix sabotaged the machines in order to be near her, even though she towered over him by at least a foot.

He would hang around her after administering his final kick, and she would humor him with a smile or an occasional kiss on his forehead. After these short moments, he would leave with a smile on his face, humming an unknown song.

Each day, Maxine would ask the guard on duty to tell the warden or whoever was in charge that she was entitled to contact the American embassy. The guard would nod and smile and say, *"Si, Señora,"* and that would be that.

One morning she composed a formal letter in Spanish—with the help of Kathy, a very thin graduate student whose boyfriend had tricked her into carrying a kilo of cocaine in her backpack—and gave it to the guard to deliver to the warden.

At 3 p.m., when the women were on a short break from their work, Gustavo, a guard they liked for his courtesy and good looks, walked over to Maxine and bent down to whisper in her ear.

"An American official is coming tomorrow to see you. Maybe in the morning. You need to be ready. Nicest clothes. Okay?"

Maxine started to cry with relief and an embarrassed Gustavo turned and walked quickly away.

Sandra stood up and glared after him. "What did that bastard say to you? Did he proposition you? Threaten you?"

"No, no, nothing like that," said Maxine. "He told me that someone from the embassy is coming to see me tomorrow. I can't believe that they listened to me, finally!"

"Don't get your hopes up, Maxine," said Darlene. "It's probably only a routine visit. I'd say that it took them long enough! That's what I would tell him!"

❧ ❧ ❧

Kurt Jenkins stood up when Maxine entered the dingy room that had been set aside for attorneys to talk to their clients. It held a table and two chairs, one on either side. A pitcher of water and two plastic cups had been placed in front of the visitor's chair, as if only he or she deserved a drink.

"Hello Ms. March. I'm Kurt Jenkins from the American embassy. How are you?" he asked, extending his hand, which she shook. Jenkins was a nice-looking and well-dressed man, probably from a family of old money and a graduate of a prestigious Ivy League college.

She sat down, as he pulled out a folder from the briefcase he had placed on the floor next to his chair.

"I've been better," she said with a sigh. "The conditions are bad in here, but I was put into what they call the international section where the women are smart and nonthreatening. They're mostly in for drug possession, many betrayed by so-called boyfriends, who often elude capture. It's a bad situation and an unjust one. I intend to write about it when . . ."

". . . you get out," said Jenkins, finishing her sentence.

"Yes, when I'm released and can return to the United States."

"I need to talk to you about that," he said.

"What did you say?" asked Maxine apprehensively. "What do you mean? I won't be getting out soon?"

"I'm afraid not, Ms. March. You are being charged with kidnapping an Ecuadorian child. The laws of this nation are very strict and harsh in a case of this kind."

Maxine felt as if she had been hit over the head. She began to shake all over, but then she took a deep breath and spoke with a steady voice.

"I did take Tito. Yes, I admit it. But he was—and is—an orphan, running in the streets with no food, no shelter, and no chance for an education. He'd probably have been coerced into joining a gang, or he might be dead by now."

"All of this is true," Jenkins replied. "You know it and I know it, at least unofficially, but the Ecuadorian government does not look at situations like this in the same way you and I look at them."

"But everything I said is true," she said, bursting into tears, then loud sobs. Jenkins got up and pulled a monogrammed handkerchief from his pocket and offered it to her. She took it and blew her nose. "Thank you."

"There will be a court hearing and, if you are bound over, a trial. I have brought you a list of good attorneys who specialize in cases like yours, I mean, where American women are caught up in the Ecuadorian justice system."

"But I have no money for an attorney!" she said. "I am a working mother. And if I don't work, I don't get paid. And what happens to Tito then?"

Jenkins stood up. "I wish I could do more. I will keep apprised of your legal status and be present at your hearings, of course." He leaned closer. "I wouldn't say much about Tito, like where he is or who is caring for him. The less said about him the better."

Maxine sat in the chair, staring at the pitcher of water, until Gustavo came in and led her back to her section. Once there, several of the women, including Dawn and Sandra, gathered around her in a group hug. When she told them what had happened, all of them started crying.

That night, a bad storm hit the prison with heavy rain, high winds, and thunder and lightning. One strike hit the main power pole and plunged several sections of the prison into darkness.

The ferocity of the storm woke Maxine up from a terrible nightmare. She and Tito were running through the jungle pursued by hooded men on giant horses with fire pouring from their mouths and nostrils. She woke up screaming and nothing Dawn or Sandra could do would quiet her. This went on for over an hour.

Finally, after many of the other inmates in the cell block shouted their complaints, two guards came in and dragged Maxine away. She kicked and screamed until one of them pulled out a large hypodermic needle and plunged it into her arm. Maxine's body went limp as she slipped into unconsciousness.

CHAPTER

THAD CALLED LORENZO while he was driving home from court. "You are set, big guy. The cases will start coming in from all directions!"

"I know it, Thad. And I owe all of it to you. Thanks very much."

"Is that all I get for what I did?" Thad said, in a serious tone.

"I don't know what you mean," said Lorenzo.

"You know exactly what I mean, big guy," said Thad, before starting to laugh. "And I do mean big!"

"Easy, easy, Thad. I'm not ready for a serious relationship with you or anyone else right now. Even though I owe you a lot, we'll have to figure out another way for me to repay you than to offer my body on the altar of lust!"

"Altar of lust!" Thad laughed. "I'd like that if I can be the high priest!"

"You're at the top of the list, believe me. Seriously, Thad, thank you."

"Okay, okay. I'll settle for dinner soon. But don't bring the kid. It kind of cramps my style."

"Agreed, just the two of us and no Tito. But you know he likes you. I could easily persuade him to call you Uncle Thaddeus."

"Spare me. I don't even get along with my sister's little brats, and I'm their real uncle," he said. "Okay, baby Renzo, gotta

go. Until soon. Need to see you. Okay?"

"Okay, Thad. Bye."

$$\text{🌿 🌿 🌿}$$

Lorenzo took Jo, Sam, and Tito out to dinner at Big River that night to celebrate his victory in court. After dinner, he dropped Jo and Sam off and drove home with Tito.

"Is my mama ever coming back to me?" Tito said suddenly.

Lorenzo hadn't said much about Maxine in the weeks she had been gone for fear of upsetting Tito. He didn't want Tito to forget her, of course, and wanted to reassure him whenever the opportunity arose. As much as he was growing to love Tito, he knew their relationship was only temporary.

"Of course, my little pal, your mama will be back to you as soon as she can. She had to go away to get permission to make you her little boy forever."

As little kids often do, Tito shrugged and didn't dwell on Lorenzo's answer. He began to talk excitedly about all he had learned from Jo as soon as they got inside the house.

"She teaches me reading, writing, and math. Even science. Let me show you my plan for a . . . what is called *experimento?*"

"An experiment. You're going to do an experiment for your study of science?"

"Yes, Papa. That's it! Let me show you." Tito ran into his room and returned with a sheet of lined notebook paper and handed it to Lorenzo. "Okay, Papa, here I go!"

Tito pulled a yellow balloon out of his pocket and blew it up. He bent over and rubbed the balloon on the carpet. Then he shoved the balloon against the wall. "See, Papa. It sticks to this wall. It is *magia!*" He clapped his hands together.

"It is magic, for certain," said Lorenzo, laughing. "It is also what is called static electricity. That means there is always electricity in the air. And when you rub it, it comes to life and reacts, like what happened with your balloon."

"Okay. Very good, Papa," said the excited little boy. "Now bend over so I can touch your hair."

Lorenzo knelt down, and Tito rubbed the balloon along his hair. It stuck and, when Lorenzo stood up, the balloon stayed in place.

"I am the balloon monster, and I'm going to get you and take you away!" he shouted, growling for good measure. The boy squealed with delight, and they ran around the room and into the hall and back again.

Lorenzo pulled the balloon from his head and sat down, out of breath.

"Do it again, Papa!" Tito shouted. "Be the balloon monster again!"

Outside in the darkness of a vehicle parked at the curb of the quiet street in northwest Corvallis, a man in a chauffeur's uniform lighted a cigarette and passed it to another man in the back seat.

"*Cigarrillo, mi patrón.*"

"*Gracias, Victorio. Vamos!*"

The car sped away. Lorenzo noticed headlights suddenly shining in the front window as the car turned around in the narrow street. But he thought nothing of it and returned to his role as the balloon monster.

CHAPTER

"TWO THINGS, LORENZO. They may be important or they might not."

Greg Nettles had called Lorenzo at home at 5 a.m. and asked to meet with him as soon as possible. They settled on McDonald Forest, the university's research forest a few miles north of town. Lorenzo had hiked there before and knew it was remote enough for private conversations, yet easily accessible to both of them since it was right off Highway 99W. Lorenzo took Tito to Jo's house on his way out of town.

Greg was already in the parking lot when Lorenzo pulled in at 8:30. Any earlier would have aroused suspicion because no students, faculty, or casual hikers would be there before daylight.

Lorenzo had picked up coffee at a drive-through place in town and handed a cup to Greg as they walked up the path for several hundred yards before spotting on an old log to sit on.

Lorenzo took a deep breath. "Boy, even a city boy like me can appreciate the glory of being in the outdoors," he said, taking a gulp of coffee. "I've got to bring Tito up here. It'll fit in perfectly with his science studies."

"He's studying science?"

"He is, with my help and Jo's. She's a really good teacher, by the way. And Sam, even though he's like a kid himself, identifies with Tito as a fellow orphan and spends

a lot of time with him."

"What about his mother, your friend who is adopting him?" asked Greg.

"Haven't heard from her in a while, but I didn't think I would. She's kind of gone undercover in Ecuador, finding out if she can adopt him there."

"But he's here," said Greg, a quizzical look on his face. "How would that work? Actually, I guess I don't want to know, working for the government as I do."

"Yeah, maybe not," said Lorenzo. "I honestly don't know what I can do for her either, except take care of the boy for now. I'm just playing it by ear."

"You ever think how you'll feel when she does come back and takes Tito away?"

"Pretty sad, no doubt about that. But we'll just have to see what happens. The main thing is that the boy is safe and secure and learning and happy, as far as I can tell."

Greg finished his coffee and crushed the cup, carefully putting the refuse in his pocket.

"Okay, Lorenzo, we can talk now. Because it is sensitive information and off the books as to my involvement, I needed this secrecy."

"I understand your position and I appreciate your help. You're a good friend and good at what you do."

"There are two things. Number one, Nick Conte is what we call an enforcer. He's the guy in the gang who carries out orders: intimidate this person, kill that person, that kind of thing. I don't know if he is actually in a gang now, but . . ."

"You mean 'gang' as in the Mafia?" asked Lorenzo.

"That's exactly what I mean."

"So, Mrs. Corning must really mean business, to bring in outside help."

Greg nodded. "I'm pretty sure he's also a muscle for hire or a gun for hire. This would be freelance stuff outside the gang. He makes extra money and keeps his skills sharp by doing things like going after people with a pickup truck. Maybe it would be bad guys he would hire. That way, he leaves no trace of himself. And he protects his clients, like your good friend Mrs. Corning. Also, a pickup truck was rented at a car rental place in Gresham on the day before the incident at the ferry. It hasn't been returned yet. Whoever rented it used a kind of funny name: Nolo Contendere."

Lorenzo laughed. "He's playing with us or whomever he thinks is on his trail. *Nolo Contendere* means 'no contest' in English and is a widely used legal term."

"Well, that fits. I mean, you being a lawyer and all."

"So you think Mrs. Corning hired him to make trouble on the case and maybe get me to back off?"

"Probably."

"But the case is over and his client lost."

"True, but his kind never gives up, so my advice to you is to watch your back—with my help, of course. I'm going to follow up on the truck rental and through some buddies in the Portland Police Department, and we'll see where that leads."

"I would love to link him to Mrs. Corning," said Lorenzo. "As a precaution against her coming back to hurt my client."

"He's still retaining you, even though you got him out of the clinic?"

"Yes, he is, and paying me a nice monthly fee. I want to help him regain control of his company. Right now, though, he just wants to reconnect with his wife and kids."

Lorenzo finished his coffee and also crushed the cup.

"What else, Greg? You said there were two things."

"Our drug gang informant, your old friend Esteban Perez, has reached out from his Witness Protection Program hideout."

"Reached out? I thought people in that program disappeared from the face of the earth."

"They're supposed to, but sometimes guys get too restless to remain under wraps forever. It means changing everything about themselves, from their name and birthday to their education and work history. We create a new life for these people, and they have to learn to live it 24 hours a day. It's easy to slip and reveal too much. It is also easy to get so bored that they return to the crime that got them into the program in the first place."

"So, what does this have to do with me?" asked Lorenzo. "I helped him and did feel he had reformed completely. Remember, he did it for his little boy. I can relate to that now, I mean because of Tito."

"Perez wants to meet with you and says he's prepared to provide us with more information about the current scene in the Pacific Northwest. Even though he's been gone for a year, he obviously keeps in touch with his old homies. How, I do not know, but these guys have their ways."

"I'll do it, both for you and for my own satisfaction to see how someone I helped recover is doing a year later. When does he want to do this?"

"How about right now?"

Lorenzo blinked. "NOW?"

Both of them turned at the sound of someone walking through the forest toward them and stood up.

"Hello, counselor," said Perez.

Without hesitation Lorenzo extended his hand. "For once in my life, I'm speechless." He turned to Greg. "I wish you had warned me."

"You're pissed," said Greg.

"Not at all. I trust you enough to know that you had your reasons."

"I never discuss sensitive stuff over the phone," he said. "I took a chance that you'd agree to see Perez and, because of what he wants to tell you, we needed to have this meeting as soon as possible."

"Fine with me," said Lorenzo, motioning toward the log that they had been sitting on. "Let's sit."

"It's your show, Perez," said Greg.

"Right, okay," said Perez. "I have done real good in my new setup. My mother and my kid are happy. She keeps up our little house and my boy goes to school, where he does real good."

"Glad to hear it, Esteban. I really am," said Lorenzo.

"I know you mean that, counselor. It's really great after what I tried to do to you." His voice trailed off.

"Go on, Perez," said Greg, impatiently. "We haven't got all day!"

Lorenzo held up his hand. "It's okay. Take your time."

"Okay, here it is straight. Some guys in my old gang are looking for me. To them, I'm a rat that must be rubbed out. They will kill me if they find me."

"So, how do I fit in?"

"Somehow they know that you were my attorney," said Perez. "So they'll try to get to me through you."

"But until now, I didn't know where you were."

"They don't know that," added Greg.

Lorenzo shook his head. "I don't want to be a decoy, even for you, Greg, or for you, Perez. It's different for me now. I have a little boy, and I'm responsible for him. Plus, I'm starting a new life here."

"You may have no choice, counselor," said Perez. "Once you're in their sights, you can't really get out of the bull's-eye."

"What have I done to my little Tito? I've put him in a bad position when I've been trying to keep him out of bad places ever since Maxine dropped him on my doorstep."

"Have you noticed anyone tailing you?" asked Greg. "People you don't know, cars you can't identify?"

"Yes! Those pickup trucks that have been trying to push me into the river or off the road."

"Pickup trucks are not their style," said Perez. "They prefer big, expensive cars."

"So, what do we do?" asked Lorenzo. "I can't put Tito or anyone near me in danger."

"They want you, not the kid or your friends," said Greg. "Let's get them away from here and then we can sort things out for you. If they are all safe, you won't worry so much. Sound okay?"

Lorenzo hesitated. "Yeah, I don't like it, but I don't have any better idea. Seems the best option, I mean, me as a decoy."

"Okay, great," said Greg. "I'll make the arrangements. We'll move the boy, your assistant, and the boy's teacher to my place at Heceta

Head. I need to do this off the books—I doubt I can get approval for us to help Perez in any way. I can send one of my best men along to protect your people. He just retired and is very discrete, so no one will know a thing about this."

"I can pay him," said Lorenzo. "I received a large retainer from the boy's mother and can certainly justify this expense." He looked at Greg and Perez. "So, we're set, right? I just want to keep my friends and myself out of harm's way, as best I can."

Then he turned to Perez. "I'm sorry you got involved in all this again. You were free and clear, but now you're right in the middle of the life you left behind."

"I want to help Agent Nettles keep you safe. He—and you—helped me a lot, and I need to return the favor. I've still got lots of information I can give you that'll probably lead to more convictions, and it'll get drugs off the street so my little boy and yours can escape that curse. Besides, I've got a few other people helping me. You won't see them, but they'll be there. Old *compadres* from my gang days."

CHAPTER

47

MAXINE WOKE UP ON A FILTHY COT in a room smelling of vomit and urine. She had no idea where she was or how long she had been there. She sensed, but could not see, other people in the room.

"You feelin' any better, honey?" said a voice. "You been out cold for a long, long time."

Maxine sat up but quickly lay down again when the room began spinning around her.

"I gots a wet rag, kind of dirty but it's wet at least."

A hand reached down and put the rag on her head. The coolness felt good.

"Thank you," Maxine said.

After a while she sat up again, this time more slowly. She swung her feet over the edge of the cot and realized that she had no shoes. And the floor felt grimy.

"Somebody always takes shoes," said the voice again. "I get you some as soon as I can."

Maxine's sight finally cleared enough for her to see the woman's face.

"Etta Mae Randolph. Pleased to make your acquaintance."

They shook hands.

"So you're the political they all talkin' about."

"Political? What do you mean?"

"It means you not in here for drugs. Most gals here either took drugs, sold drugs, or carried drugs out of this country."

"And you?"

"I rather not say at this time. We don't know each other that long."

"I understand," said Maxine. "I didn't mean to be so nosey, but can I ask you how long you've been here?"

"Almost a year. My lawyer say I can get out after a year is up, but I don't trust him. He took all I had as his pay—jewelry mostly and some nice clothes," said Etta Mae. "But let's talk about helpin' you. It takes some getting' used to in here. I won't lie to you. It's a hellhole, that's for sure. You get along better with a protector. I guess that's me. But don't get me wrong, I don't want to have sex with you or get money from you. I just want someone to have a decent conversation with. And maybe, if you get out before me, some help in lettin' people know where I am. I mean my mama and my little girl, mostly."

"How old is she?"

"Blossom is seven." Etta Mae pulled a wrinkled photo out of a pocket. "She a sweetie, don't you think? What about you, honey? What's a nice white lady like you doin' in a rotten place like this?"

Maxine liked Etta Mae, but she had only known her for a few minutes. She decided to tell her just enough to stay on her good side but not enough to compromise herself later.

"I'm trying to adopt a little boy from Ecuador, and everything got fouled up," she said. "It's real complicated. I didn't have the right kind of permit, and I didn't show up for an appointment and all kinds of things like that. So the officials threw me in jail for the time being. At least, I hope it's only for the time being! I got sick and was hallucinating and making a fuss so they drugged me and threw me in here, but I should be out soon."

"Maybe yes, maybe no," Etta Mae said. "They kinda' forget folks once in a while."

Maxine felt a chill go up and down her spine, but she kept her composure.

Etta Mae stood up. "Okay, first thing I do is to get you some shoes. Stay sittin' there while I see what I can do in that department." She started to walk away but turned around. "You got any money?"

"It's hidden in my shopping bag, but they took it away when I was brought in."

"Reason I asked is you need money to buy food. Otherwise, all you get in here is rice and sardines. But when you get your food, you gotta be careful and keep it away from the rats—some of them is as big as rabbits!"

"Sounds horrible," said Maxine, sticking out her tongue as if to gag. "I've never had a sardine in my life! And I've never seen a rat, except in a college science course!"

"I wouldn't know about some college. Sardines is cheap and so is rice," said Etta Mae. "I guess that's why it's all they give us. But with money, you can buy canned meat and crackers and maybe some fruit and cheese. Tea and coffee? They're extra. It's all what they call contraband but they allow us to buy it, maybe so they don't have to buy so much rice and sardines."

"Would you take an IOU for whatever you spend on food for me?"

"Sure, honey. I'll do that."

"I'll pay for food for both of us and give you even more, as soon as I get my money."

"Okay. It's a deal. Let me go and take care of all of this for you."

Maxine remained on the cot and closed her eyes in a vain effort to shut out her horrible surroundings.

After a while, she heard a tiny voice near her face. "You are pretty. Are you a movie star?"

Maxine opened her eyes to see a girl of twelve or so standing in front of her with a big smile on her face.

"I'm Nola," she said. "Pleased to meet you." The girl was wearing a dirty dress, and she smelled as if she hadn't had a bath in many days. "My mama is in this jail, like you."

A thin young woman wearing a faded smock and worn tennis shoes walked toward her. "There are about sixty kids in this prison," she said. "We mothers do our best to keep them safe and fed, but it's hard. Name's Valerie Ambrose."

They shook hands, and she sat down on the cot next to Maxine. The little girl snuggled in beside her.

"They keep talking about setting up a school and providing milk for the kids, but nothing happens."

"But can't you and Nola at least get moved to the other section where conditions are a bit better?"

"Not yet. My boyfriend Roger got caught for smuggling guns to the rebels. He did it on a dare, when he was high. I was there too, drinking and smoking dope like crazy. Now he's in a super max prison in the Andes, and I'm here. They say I'm a flight risk so here I sit. I got used to it a while ago, but I hate it for Nola. This'll leave a mark on her forever."

"So Valerie's been tellin' you her tale of woe," said Etta Mae as she walked up to the cot. "That's okay, girl, I know it's all true."

Etta Mae placed a pair of combat boots on the floor in front of Maxine. Next from a large bag came a wool sweater, two pairs of jeans, two sweatshirts, some socks, and bras and panties.

"Not sure of your breast size," she said, eyeing Maxine closely. "I mean, it's hard to tell how big they are under that awful outfit you got on."

"I'm pretty flat-chested," said Maxine.

"So, here's what we'll do. I'll stand guard while you take a shower, and then you can put on clean clothes. You'll feel a lot better. Okay, honey? I pay off the women who look after the shower, so you'll be safe."

"Sounds wonderful to me."

Valerie and Nola sat there, watching as Maxine took off all her clothes and left them in a pile on the cot.

"Why don't you come with me, and we'll all shower together. Three for the price of one. Right, Etta Mae? You can leave your clothes on, if you want, and just enjoy the water."

They walked into the showers, which were in an equally filthy room down the corridor. Soon sounds of splashing water and laughter echoed through the room—both a rarity in this gruesome place.

🌿 🌿 🌿

Later that night things got decidedly worse. Maxine was awakened by clanging keys and shuffling feet. She opened her eyes and saw what appeared to be a soldier pointing both a flashlight and a rifle in her face.

"*Despertarse!*" he shouted.

She sat up and the man yanked her to her feet. As she tried to wake up, a large woman in a uniform walked over and slapped her.

"Is this the Yankee terrorist who kidnaps our babies?"

"*Si, mi general.*"

"Get her out of here, *pronto.*"

At that, soldiers dragged Maxine out of the room, down the corridor, and into a cell. When the iron door clanged shut, darkness engulfed her.

CHAPTER

TWO DAYS PASSED and Lorenzo went about the business of working on the new cases that had been referred to him by other attorneys. They ranged from a fairly simple patent infringement to a more complicated custody battle over a prize-winning show dog. In every instance, Sam did a thorough job of researching the pertinent case law and typing up the briefs that they needed to file with the appropriate courts.

"Sam, please come in here and sit down," Lorenzo called from his office.

"What did I do, boss? Whatever it is, I can make it up to you, I know I can."

Lorenzo's face looked stern, and he put his hand to his head and sighed. Sam looked as if he was going to faint.

"It has come to my attention . . ." Lorenzo paused for effect, ". . . that you have been working much too hard, and I want to give you a weekend off, all expenses paid at my friend Greg's house on the coast. Tito and Jo will go too. And I'm going to give you a raise. We've been making good money, and I want to share it with you because you have played a big role in making this all happen."

Sam got a huge grin on his face. "Oh my, boss! Thanks a lot. You are a great boss and a great friend. But you scared the you-know-what out of me!" he said. Then as an afterthought, "Can't you go too?"

"No, I've got too much work to do. I just want you guys to go and have a good time. Okay, kid, it's time to get back to work!"

🌿 🌿 🌿

At home, later that evening, Lorenzo packed clothes and toys for Tito and the food he had asked Sam to buy at Trader Joe's, then waited by his front door. Twenty minutes later, a black SUV rounded the corner of the block and pulled up in the driveway. A tall man of about sixty got out and walked up to the door.

"Mr. Madrid, I'm MacIntosh Dunnigan," he said in a quiet voice. "My friends call me Mack. Agent Nettles has briefed me and given me directions to his place. I can take it from here."

He knelt in front of Tito, who was standing behind Lorenzo and looking a bit frightened.

"Hi Tito," he said with a smile. "My name is Mack."

Lorenzo said to Tito, "Jo and Sam are in the car, little man. You're all going with Mack back to the coast and that lighthouse you saw before. Remember?"

Tito took Mack's hand and walked solemnly down the walkway to the car. Once there, the rear door flew open and Sam stepped out.

"Is that my little brown friend?" he said, laughing. He picked Tito up and whirled him around.

"And you are my favorite Black friend," replied Tito. "We are buddies."

Then Jo peeked her head out of the passenger door, winked at Tito, and said, "Won't you come into my magic carriage?"

Tito squealed with delight and jumped in. The car backed out and drove off. Lorenzo was still waving long after it had disappeared around the corner.

🌿 🌿 🌿

The next day, Lorenzo kept a long-standing invitation to give a talk to a class at the Willamette College of Law. Because it was not a formal lecture, he could keep it casual. Thad Sampson, who had arranged it, went with him. A few people not in the class sat in the rear of the auditorium.

"We are honored today to have a distinguished attorney speak to our class," said the professor, an older man who wore the classic tweed jacket with leather patches on the elbows. Lorenzo bet he smoked a pipe as well. "He has had a very successful career here in Oregon and in California, where he taught at the UCLA School of Law. He has recently returned to Oregon to set up his own practice in Corvallis. I give you Lorenzo Madrid."

A smattering of applause followed. Lorenzo had learned in his classes at UCLA that you had to earn applause and respect from students. They usually didn't even crack a smile at his jokes until a month into the course.

"Thank you, Professor Sanders. I am happy to be here today to talk about an area of the law you may not know much about but one that is more vital today than at any other time in our recent history. That would be immigration law."

For the next hour, Lorenzo discussed the current state of immigration law—how cases were handled, and how attorneys dealt with the often desperate people who came to them.

"Things have changed for the worse since the new president took office. He is carrying out a Draconian policy of roundup and deport. Often the people who get picked up are guilty of nothing more than wanting a better life. He has instilled a fear of what I call 'the other' among the largely white people who elected him. This will end badly, not only for the people caught in this horrible trap but also for our American democracy."

Now the students not only applauded him but stood to do so.

Even as he acknowledged the applause, Lorenzo could not help but notice the well-dressed Hispanic who walked out of the auditorium, followed at a respectful distance by a grim-looking man.

CHAPTER

MAXINE HAD CRIED SO MUCH that exhaustion had eventually over-whelmed her body, and she had fallen into a deep sleep. The sound of the iron door creaking open woke her up, but the complete darkness of the cell made it impossible for her to know whether it was day or night.

"*Señora* March. You must wake up. We must go." The voice was familiar, but she couldn't see the face that went with it. Gentle hands helped her stand up on her wobbly legs. "Here, put this on."

The man handed her fresh clothes and turned his back while she changed into them. She could tell by the smells wafting from her body that she had soiled herself.

"Oh, my God, I am a mess!" she wailed.

The man helped her walk out of the isolation cell and into the cor-ridor. As they walked, she saw that her savior was Gustavo, the friendly guard who had helped her many times since she first arrived at the prison.

"I'm taking you back to the first place they put you. You have been in solitary confine-ment for one day with no food and very little water. We must get you some help."

"Who was that awful woman who put me in the black hole? Why did she do that to me?"

Gustavo led her to a chair and answered,

"That was General Violetta Braganza, the only woman general we have in the Ecuadorian army. She hates Americans because her only son was killed in a raid led by your special forces several years ago. They were trying to capture members of a drug cartel at their jungle headquarters."

"And an American soldier shot him?"

Gustavo nodded his head in dismay. "Yes, I am afraid so. Since then, she becomes irrational when she encounters an American."

"Will she return and throw me in the black hole again?"

"It is not likely. She was just passing through here, and she happened to hear about you. That's why she lashed out. She usually sticks to her desk job in army headquarters in Quito."

Maxine exhaled. "That's a relief."

Gustavo helped Maxine stand up. "Let's get you back to your friends."

Down another long corridor and through two sets of iron doors and they were back to the area where Maxine had been put when she first arrived.

"*Señoras y señoritas,*" yelled Gustavo. "I have a surprise for you!"

"What the hell?" complained Dawn. "Can't a girl get any sleep at all around here?"

"Hello, Dawn," said Maxine. "I'm home."

Gustavo unlocked the door and Maxine walked in.

"Well, look who's here!" said Sandra.

"Come in, baby," said Dawn. "We'll get you back to normal as fast as we can, if anything can ever be normal in this godforsaken place!"

Maxine was very grateful for their kindness. Although she hadn't known these women long, they were the only friends she had now.

CHAPTER

EXCEPT FOR THE OCCASIONAL ROUTINE PATROL looking for drug-growing plantations and drug smugglers, DeStefano and his squad spent a lot of time just hanging out. So he made the men clean their weapons daily and work out all the time, "just in case."

The call from the embassy a few weeks before had sent them on a rare mission. Although he had been given few details, DeStefano guessed that the whole enterprise had been political. They were not looking for lost tourists or American bad guys escaping the U.S. Marshal Service. The woman they had just missed was being held by the Ecuadorian government.

A week later, just after the squad had returned from a routine night patrol and were eating supper, a loud knock at the door interrupted their casual banter. Benny Porten, the medic, got up to answer it.

Paul Bickford had always been one of those men whose presence could easily fill a room and drown out everyone and everything in it. "WHICH ONE OF YOU FUCKERS IS DESTEFANO?" he shouted.

"That would be me, sir." DeStefano stood up and extended his hand.

Bickford ignored the gesture. "We need to figure out how we're going to rescue an American lady from the hellhole of

A LORENZO MADRID MYSTERY

a prison your incompetence put her into!"

DeStefano's face turned red, and he got up close to Bickford. "Begging your pardon, SIR, but we did not screw up! We got to that jail in less than an hour after we got the call from the embassy. The Ecuadorians were just faster. What can I say?"

Bickford sat down and took off his helmet. He looked exhausted. "Water. Got any water? For my men too."

Porten handed Bickford a water bottle and he drank it dry. The others did the same. Then he turned his attention back to DeStefano.

"What you *can* say is how we're going to get her out of there."

"I haven't had any orders to engage in that kind of mission," said DeStefano. "I work for the American embassy, not you."

Several of his men gasped at their leader's audacity.

Bickford stood up and walked over to DeStefano, who was powerfully built but stood shorter than the colonel. As a result, Bickford easily looked down at DeStefano.

"What's your rank?"

"Captain, sir."

"Glad you threw that 'sir' in, captain. You know what insubordination is?"

"Disobeying a superior officer, for one thing," said DeStefano.

"Damn right," said Bickford, relaxing a bit and signaling for more water. "Okay, here's what I hope we can do together. I would like you and your men to do a recon job for me. Find out all you can about the prison at Guayaquil. Where it is, what is around it, like any other buildings or open spaces. Find out who the guards are, I mean, what part of the government—military, private, locals—they are from. Locals are easier to deal with than federal, but they're all susceptible to bribery. Show me a cop south of the border who is not willing to take money under the table to do whatever you want, and I'll buy you a case of tequila."

DeStefano relaxed a bit when he saw Bickford's confrontational style ease up.

"I mean no disrespect, sir, but is any of this authorized? I mean by the U.S. government?"

Bickford shook his head. "No, but it should be. The government of the strongest country the world has ever seen should not stand by when any of its citizens are in harm's way. I'm being investigated right now—that's nothing new. I've always operated off the books, so to speak, so I think my bosses in Special Ops will view anything we do as permitted under our loose rules. Our job has always been to do whatever it takes to protect American interests overseas. In my view, rescuing an American citizen protects our interests."

DeStefano didn't say anything at first. He stared at Bickford and then his men, all of whom looked like they were tired of being idle and wanted to see some action.

"You've got our backs, sir? I don't know about you, but I've got only five years to go until I can retire with full bennies and quit doing all this fun stuff and sit around all day drinkin' with my lady."

"You have my word as an officer in the United States Army. I may not look it today, but I clean up well. And what's more, I've got some juice where it counts. I know where lots of bodies are buried."

"Okay then," DeStefano said to his men. "Let's do this thing and do it right!" He turned to Bickford. "What's your lady's name?"

"I wouldn't say she's . . ."

"Sir, let's be honest," said DeStefano.

"Okay, okay. You got me," said Bickford. "My lady. But there's also the welfare of a little boy that you'd all love."

"Benny, do the honors," ordered DeStefano.

The medic got up and walked to a locked cabinet and took out a full bottle of whiskey. He filled a dozen paper cups and passed them around.

"What's your friend's name?" asked DeStefano.

"Maxine."

"And the boy?"

"Tito."

"Okay, you rat fuckers," shouted DeStefano, "a toast to Maxine!"

They touched each other's cups and hoisted them in the air.

"To Maxine!"
"Now the boy," said DeStefano.
"To Tito."

CHAPTER

AT 2:15 THAT MORNING, Lorenzo was awakened by loud knocking on his front door. He put on a sweatshirt and rushed to answer it, stubbing his toe on a table along the way.

"Greg! What is it? Something happen to Tito?"

Greg rushed in. "I got a call! Something's not right!"

"Where? You mean at your house on the coast?" Lorenzo led Greg to the couch. "Sit down and take some deep breaths. Here's some water."

Greg emptied the glass in one gulp.

"Okay, now tell me what you're talking about. Who did you get a call from? Mack, the guy who's watching my kid?"

"Yeah, about an hour ago. Took me that long to get here. He sounded terrible, said someone was trying to get into the house and was shooting at them."

"Oh, God, no!" said Lorenzo, an anguished look on his face. "I'm supposed to be taking care of him. God, if anything happens to him, I'll want to die too."

"Lorenzo, calm down. Sit down. We both can't be in hysterics," said Greg. "We don't know what's happening yet. I've called in all my chits. There's the state police, the county sheriff, and some of my DEA guys on the way."

"We need to get over there too!" said Lorenzo. "I can't wait here for a phone call that tells me Tito and the others are dead. I can't sit here doing nothing!"

"I agree," said Greg. "Get dressed, and we'll get out to the Corvallis airport."

"Airport? Corvallis has an airport?" said Lorenzo.

"I've got a helicopter waiting to get us to Florence and a car there to take us to the cabin."

"I am impressed . . . and grateful," said Lorenzo.

"I told you I called in lots of chits."

❦ ❦ ❦

Esteban Perez had been watching Greg's cabin for hours. His DEA protector had loaned him his second car to use while he was in Oregon. He had driven to Newport and spent several days sightseeing. Men on the run never have the time for sightseeing. Nor do drug lords, he thought. He had figured out that whoever was after Lorenzo Madrid would hit him where he was most vulnerable—by kidnapping or killing the boy.

Perez admired Madrid for his legal skills and his willingness to forget their fractured past and meet with him and help him once again. He owed him for his freedom and the chance to live quietly with his son and his mother. He could understand Lorenzo's love for the boy. What he could not understand was how such an intelligent and handsome man could ever be attracted only to other men. He had once used the Spanish word *maricón* to describe him and he regretted that now that he knew him. He shook his head at the thought of not having sex with women or the ability to have a son or daughter of his own.

"No comprendo," he said with a shrug and continued to watch the cabin below.

CHAPTER

THE SUN WAS JUST RISING as the helicopter landed at the tiny airport in Florence. Lorenzo and Greg ducked down to avoid the whirling rotors as they got off because the pilot would not be shutting down the engines. A car was parked near the small building that served as the waiting room and operations center.

"Thanks, Joe," yelled Nettles to a man standing in the door. "I owe you."

The man nodded and walked inside.

Greg and Lorenzo got into the nondescript government sedan and Greg turned on the ignition. He turned north on Highway 101, the main north/south route that went from border to border.

"Is there a plan?" asked Lorenzo.

"Are you kidding?" said Greg. "If I have learned anything else in my long years with the DEA, it's that we usually have to improvise like hell in almost everything we do."

They drove in silence for several miles. Lorenzo could feel his body tense up with every mile the car traveled. Tito's welfare was all he could think about. Inevitably, he felt a lot of guilt for putting this innocent little boy in danger.

"We're almost at the tunnel," said Greg.

"Feel like taking a little hike? I'm going to pull over here and leave the car. We don't want to announce ourselves until we're ready."

He backed the car as far into the underbrush as he could, and they got out. They were opposite the place on 101 where a large pullout allowed people to view the Heceta Head Lighthouse from a half-mile away, perched on a shelf overlooking the Pacific Ocean. This iconic view of the lighthouse had been on the cover of many books and magazines and printed on postcards. Tourists lined up every day to take the perfect shot of family members or friends with the lighthouse in the background.

Lorenzo and Greg had no time for such a diversion.

"We've got to go through the tunnel," Greg shouted over his shoulder. "Probably won't be any cars or trucks coming through this early."

They started jogging. At about the halfway point, they saw the headlights of a truck just entering the tunnel at a high speed. Logging trucks were notorious for speeding along this highway during the night when no police or other vehicles were around to slow them down.

With the speeding truck fast approaching, Lorenzo and Greg flattened themselves against the slimy wall of the tunnel. Although the truck missed them, Lorenzo felt the wind from the truck blast through his hair and clothes.

After the truck had passed, they resumed their jog.

"Whew!" said Greg. "To say that was a close call would be an understatement!"

They continued along the highway to a point just south of the driveway to Greg's house. Greg signaled Lorenzo to move into the brush.

"Where's our backup?" whispered Lorenzo.

"That's what I want to know!" said Greg.

He pointed up the hill, and they started to climb through the bramble of salal and blackberry bushes and other undergrowth. After a few hundred yards, he stopped and held up his hand.

The darkened house was straight ahead, with no signs of life in or around it. Greg motioned for Lorenzo to walk along one side of the house while he walked up to the other. He pulled out a gun. Greg's eyes widened when Lorenzo did the same, but he said nothing.

Lorenzo chanced a quick look in the kitchen window. In the weak light of dawn, he could see inside. At first, it appeared to be empty, and then he saw a man's body lying on the floor.

"Please, don't let it be Sam," he muttered to himself.

Just then, the front door burst open and Greg rushed in, crouching low. As he did, Lorenzo ran around to the same door and into the house. Lorenzo pointed toward where he had seen the man, and Greg moved in that direction. Lorenzo followed.

Greg shined a light on the face. "It's Mack." He felt for a pulse and shook his head. Up close, Lorenzo could see a bullet hole in his chest.

Greg pointed up the stairs and both of them headed up. The doors to the bedrooms were all closed. Greg and Lorenzo opened the first two so fast that they hit the walls behind them and bounced back. Both rooms were empty.

Lorenzo opened the door to the third bedroom slowly, expecting to have to dodge a fist or a bullet. Instead, he saw Jo sitting on the floor, tied up and gagged.

Lorenzo rushed over to her and removed the gag. She coughed and started to cry.

"Oh, Lorenzo, it was terrible! These awful men came and shot at the house, and Mr. Mack got hit. I fear he is dead. Such a kind man. And then . . ."

"And then what?" asked an anguished Lorenzo.

"They took the boy." She was sobbing loudly now. "I'm so sorry. I let you down, and I let Tito down!"

He bent down and held her in his arms. "It's okay," he said softly. "I'm sure everything will be okay." He looked around the room, expecting to see someone else tied up or dead. "Where's Sam? What happened to Sam?"

"They beat him up pretty badly and then your little boy threw himself onto him, to try to protect him."

"And then?" Lorenzo asked quickly.

"They stopped hitting him and took Tito and Sam with them, to

God-only-knows-where."

"How many of them were there?" asked Greg.

"Two came in here, real thugs they were. One Spanish looking and the other a smaller man, maybe Italian from the look of him."

"Maybe Nick Conte," said Lorenzo.

"Could be the driver of the limo you keep seeing," said Greg. He turned to Jo. "Anything else you can tell us?"

"I glanced out the window at one point and saw a rather elegantly dressed man standing in the yard," she said. "It was dark, of course, but Mack had turned the flood lights on, so I could see him fairly clearly."

"You have a remarkable ability to recall people you've seen only briefly," said Greg.

"It's because you learned to look carefully at everyone in London at the time of the IRA," she said. "You can't be completely afraid, of course, or you wouldn't ever leave your house. I suspect Londoners are feeling that now, with all the terrorists about."

"You rest here for a while, and we'll be back soon," said Lorenzo, as he and Greg headed out the door.

CHAPTER

53

BICKFORD, DESTEFANO, AND THEIR MEN rode in a convoy of Humvees to a clearing in the jungle a mile away from the prison. DeStefano signaled when to stop and got out of the vehicle. He motioned for Bickford to join him at his vehicle and spread out what looked like maps and floor plans on the hood.

"This is it," he said. "The formal name of the prison is Litoral, why I do not know. It's not like any prison in the U.S. of A, that's for sure. It is a mix of brick and cement buildings and a series of shacks that look like they're going to fall down at any minute. Everything in that place is governed by bribes. You pay the right people and you get better food, nicer living conditions, stuff like that. If you can't pay—and most Ecuadorians cannot—you are put in Pavilion Three, which is dirty and rat-infested and much more dangerous. Our guy on the inside does not know where she is. It's a big place, so it'll be tough to find her."

"She's in with other women?"

"Yeah, the women are kept separate from the men, but conjugal visits are allowed. Over 1,000 guys and an estimated 300 women are in there, plus about 60 children."

"Children in a prison! That's really shitty," Bickford said, shaking his head in disbelief. "So what's your plan, DeStefano?"

"I sent word to our informant inside. He's a guard, and we pay him well to watch over the American women and their kids who are in there. We wait here until midmorning, when he makes a mail run, and he'll stop here to give us a report."

"Seems pretty casual to me," said Bickford, "but it's your show, and I appreciate all you're doing. We'll let it play out."

With a mix of men from both units standing guard, Bickford and DeStefano both got some much needed shuteye.

An hour later, Porten touched DeStefano's shoulder to wake him up. "He's here, boss."

Bickford woke up too and stood up.

A Hispanic man in a guard's uniform stepped forward and extended his hand.

DeStefano shook his hand and introduced him. "This is our good friend Gustavo. He's been helping us for many years."

"*Mucho gusto, señor.*"

"On behalf of the United States government, I want to thank you for your work," Bickford said.

DeStefano leaned forward and whispered in Bickford's ear. "Cut the crap, colonel. He's helping us, sure, but he is also being paid well."

"A little 'crap,' as you call it, never hurts," Bickford whispered back. He turned to Gustavo. "Have you seen my good friend, Maxine March?"

Gustavo nodded vigorously. "Yes, many times I have seen her. She's a very nice lady. Very scared now. I help her when I can. Not easy but I help her."

"Tell us everything you can about her and where she is in the prison—I mean the location," said Bickford, pointing to the map.

Gustavo moved over to look at it and pointed to a spot about half-way in from the outer wall.

"She is here, in this location," he said. "She was put in isolation last week. Into a black hole with no food and not much water."

"Oh God! Poor Maxine!"

"The next day, I went there to take some food to her," Gustavo continued. "No guards were around, so I returned her to the original cell where she had made some friends."

"Just like that? No guards in this maximum security place?" said DeStefano. "Shit, what a joke!"

"This was in an old section of the prison that is not staffed now. A general came through—a woman general—and she got very mad at *Señora* March and put her in that place."

"Why so angry at someone she did not even know?"

"Because she say that *Señora* March kidnapped a little boy from my country and took him to the United States."

Bickford shook his head. "It's not true but not important now, I guess. So, she's back in an area that is not very secure?"

"Yes, that is where she is."

They talked with Gustavo a long time and found out the routines of guards, the locations of interior and exterior doors, and the kinds of guns used to guard against escapes.

After an hour, Gustavo looked at his watch and stood up. "I need to go, *señores. Muchas gracias. Buena suerte.*"

DeStefano pulled out a stack of one hundred dollar bills and handed them to Gustavo.

"*Muchas gracias* to you!"

🌿 🌿 🌿

They waited for twilight and then moved out on foot toward the prison, about a mile away. Bickford and DeStefano, understandably vying for supremacy, led the way, at times jockeying for lead position on the narrow trail.

The road ended at the outer wall of the prison, and they fanned out in two directions, always staying in the jungle for protection. Consulting the guard rotation schedule Gustavo had given them, Bickford pointed to his watch and then held up ten fingers to indicate the time remaining before the incursion.

Bickford and DeStefano pulled off their military jumpsuits, revealing the white cotton pants and shirt and colorful wool vest of a peasant. They also put on hats and fake moustaches.

"Ready, DeStefano?"
"Ready, sir."

CHAPTER

AS LORENZO AND GREG RAN DOWN THE ROAD into the state park, shots rang out from above, in the direction of the lighthouse.

"Let's go!" shouted Lorenzo as he headed through the parking lot and up the hill. They were both out of breath when they reached the top and ran past the keeper's house.

"Stop right there, you bastard!" yelled a voice.

Nick Conte was standing at the edge of the cliff on the other side of the fence holding a screaming Tito under one arm. Another man was standing over Sam, who was lying on the ground, not moving.

"Papa! Help me!"

Conte reached around and slapped him. "Shut up, you little half-breed!"

Lorenzo started walking very slowly toward the men, with Greg, out of sight behind some bushes, circling around to his right.

"I don't get it, Conte," Lorenzo said. "Why are you doing this? I imagine Mrs. Corning paid you well for your services. Her stepson got out of the clinic, true, but that wasn't your fault."

"But you made it happen," he said. "You messed up my plans. You made me look bad when you didn't get scared off!" The usually cold and composed Conte was looking a bit confused. "I loved her," he blurted.

"She told me she'd marry me if I got rid of her stepson. She's old but she liked the sex with me. I figured . . ."

"You figured that an occasional roll in the hay with her, as distasteful as it was, would set you up for life," Lorenzo said. "You are a fool!"

"Okay, okay. Maybe so. But you rubbed me the wrong way too, with your high and mighty ways. You think you're better than people like me."

Lorenzo snickered. "It's people like me who get people like you out of trouble."

"I wouldn't hire a greaser like you to shine my shoes."

"So, I see it's a racial thing," said Lorenzo. "Your loss, *amigo.*"

"USE ENGLISH!"

"But why go after my kid?" asked Lorenzo. "Andy Corning's got two kids. She could have had you take them."

"She hates you for showing her up in court," he said. "We checked you out and found out about this kid and how you're taking care of him."

Conte moved closer to the edge and began to dangle Tito by his legs.

"Papa, Papa! Help me!"

Just then a shot rang out and hit Conte in the arm. As he whirled away from the bullet, Lorenzo rushed in, snatched Tito in his arms, and ran back toward the lighthouse. Conte aimed a gun at them, but before he could pull the trigger, another shot hit him in the head and he fell to the ground. Another shot hit the other thug in the chest and he fell over.

"Papa, Papa," sobbed Tito. "You have saved me."

"You bet I did, little man," said Lorenzo, tears welling up in his eyes. "You bet I did." He kissed Tito and carried him over to a bench away from Conte's body.

"Look who I found, passed out over there," said Greg. He was helping Sam limp over to them.

"Drinking on the job again, Sammy?" joked Lorenzo to ease the tension.

"No, no, Papa. Sam was brave and saved me and even got knocked down by that bad guy. He was very brave. Don't be mad at him, Papa."

Lorenzo frowned for a second and then smiled. "Come here, my good friend."

Sam hobbled over to them and sat on the bench. They all put their arms around one another.

High on the hill above it all, Esteban Perez wiped his fingerprints off the handle of his high-powered rifle and threw it as far as he could into the pounding sea.

"*Tranquilo!*" he said, before turning and walking back into the forest.

🌿 🌿 🌿

When Bickford and DeStefano walked calmly through the front door of the prison—as Gustavo had convinced them that it was safe to do—they were met by a volley of shots from the rifles of a line of Ecuadorian soldiers. Both fell to the ground, bleeding from multiple wounds.

A man dressed in an officer's uniform walked over to them and kicked them onto their backs to view their faces more clearly.

"*Gringos!*" said Major Francisco Manteca. "They think they own the world!"

Meanwhile, in a drab and dingy cell in another part of the massive prison, Maxine March woke up to another day of hopelessness.

The End